"You were going to call me Alex."

He stopped in his tracks and looked down at her questioningly.

"I decided against it," Agnes replied tartly, "in case you thought I was getting too familiar."

"I'm not averse to familiarity—with the right person." His eyes held amusement in their depths, and he studied her speculatively.

"And what are your views on the subject of marriage?"

"It may surprise you to learn that not all women think that marriage is the prize at the end of the race," Agnes told him with the hint of challenge in her eyes. "We're capable of leading independent lives, although that's not to say I'm against marriage."

"You reassure me," Alex drawled.

JACQUELINE GILBERT began writing for the Harlequin Presents series in 1976. She has since written approximately one romance novel a year, a pace that allows her a good deal of time to devote to her family. "In the final analysis," she says, "the family is the only stable and significant thing in our lives." She and her husband, the person she credits most for helping her to become the person she is today, live in England's Midlands and count themselves lucky to have both children and grandchildren.

Books by Jacqueline Gilbert

JACQUELINE GILBERT

Once in a Lifetime

Harlequin Books

TORONTO • NEW YORK • LONDON
AMSTERDAM • PARIS • SYDNEY • HAMBURG
STOCKHOLM • ATHENS • TOKYO • MILAN
MADRID • WARSAW • BUDAPEST • AUCKLAND

For John

Harlequin Presents first edition October 1992
ISBN 0-373-11497-4

Original hardcover edition published in 1991
by Mills & Boon Limited

ONCE IN A LIFETIME

CHAPTER ONE

A TWO-SEATER Morgan, painted sunflower-yellow, was travelling north from Edinburgh with its owner singing at the top of her voice, the tune snatched away by the wind, which was also playing havoc with her hair, tossing and twisting it as she sped along.

Agnes Quinn felt her spirits rising as each mile passed. She had had a busy week, clearing her desk, appointment book and drawing-board of the most important items of work, and was now escaping to her beloved Ardneath. For a while at least she could put her problems behind her.

Still warbling, she feasted her eyes on the hazy grey-purple mountains and assessed the sky with a practised eye. The fine spell, she decided, wouldn't last long.

But it would take more than a change in the weather to dampen her spirits. She was bound for a small cottage on the banks of Loch Rhu, Ardneath, the place of her childhood. It was primitive by modern day standards, with water pumped from a well and oil lamps for light, but Agnes found no difficulty in adapting to the simple life at Cluny Cottage—in fact, that was part of its charm, together with the beautiful Highland countryside in which it was placed.

'"But my false lover stole the rose. . ."' crooned Agnes, revelling in the drama of the romantic ballad, when she heard something that instantly and abruptly cut the flow. The Morgan had given an ominous cough.

She screwed up her face in concentration, listening intently to the sound of the engine, her eyes flicking to the dials on the dashboard. Nothing seemed to be amiss there. She relaxed slightly and for some seconds everything was serene and then the Morgan coughed again, shuddered, and the engine cut out completely.

Agnes swore in disgust, and allowed the car to drift to the bottom of an incline, where it gently rested its four wheels.

'Ah, come on now,' she cajoled as she turned the key in the ignition, getting no response. The sky was changing. Clouds were forming rapidly and the wind had grown cooler; rummaging in a holdall, Agnes pulled out a sweater, and, thrusting herself out of the car, she shrugged it on over the shirt and voluminous skirt she was wearing. She then set about putting up the Morgan's soft top, making it secure, and when that was done she felt ready to tackle, hopefully, the reason why it had given up the ghost.

She lifted up the two-sided bonnet, one side after the other, studying the engine and all its bits and pieces carefully. Frowning as she drew a blank, Agnes went over it all again, but still with no luck. Giving an exasperated sigh she banged down the bonnet and glared at the Morgan—her pride and joy. She then glanced eagerly up and down the road, for once not appreciating the stark grandeur of the mountains surrounding her on all sides. There was not a soul in sight.

'Shall I wait, or walk?' she wondered, addressing the Morgan as it sat smugly resplendent in polished glory. Agnes searched her memory and reckoned that the next garage was at least five miles further on. She gave a dour look at the sky and decided it would be more sensible to stay and wait in the car.

'Someone will come by sooner or later,' she reflected optimistically and climbed in, ducking her head under the soft top, settling herself comfortably for a long wait.

She put her arms across the steering-wheel and rested her chin on her hands. Every now and then she glanced at the rear-view mirror and out at the road ahead, but both were disappointingly empty.

She wasn't particularly worried. Not yet. She had been used to standing on her own two feet for a long time and was responsible to no one but herself.

Again her eyes focused on the mirror; she also took in her own appearance and gave a spurt of laughter. An open-topped sports car definitely encouraged the tousled look! Although she had a comb in her bag she wasn't moved to do anything about it.

Agnes Quinn had a pert attractiveness made up

of large tawny eyes, well-spaced and lashed, a nose that tilted slightly at the tip and had a light sprinkling of freckles from the summer's sun, a mobile mouth and a pointed chin. All these features gave indications of a sense of humour and a strength of purpose, and the level, thoughtful gaze intimated a degree of intelligence. Her hair was her crowning glory, being abundant, thick and strong with a natural wave. It was all shades of blonde and today was caught up from the sides in a giant bulldog clip, but any stylish effect had been drastically reduced by the battering it had taken. As might be supposed of someone who had studied art and textile design, her clothes were eye-catching and her slightly above average height allowed her to carry them off.

She had had no real problems in her life until recently, only the small annoyances which someone who was running her own business had to expect. Anastasia Designs—her mother had been deeply into Russian history when deciding on a second name for her daughter—was gradually becoming recognised and interesting work was coming her way. But the building where she lived and worked had just been sold to an investment company and the new owners wanted her out as soon as possible. They were prepared to buy up the remainder of her lease—the two other apartments were already empty—but so far she had refused their offer. She had put a great deal of hard work into making the studio right and she had no intention of leaving. Let them force her out if they could! However much money was on offer, she wasn't prepared to consider the hassle of moving in somewhere else—an awesome thought.

Agnes put her problem from her mind as a loud rumbling in her stomach reminded her she hadn't eaten since breakfast. Her watch told her that half an hour had gone very slowly. And then she heard it. The distant hum of a vehicle coming up fast. She fought with the handle and in a frenzy of energy leaped from the Morgan. She hit her shin, cursing under her breath as she raced up the grassy bank bordering the road and waved both arms wildly in the air, waiting eagerly for the car to appear.

The hum became louder and then a white shape topped the brow of the hill and came, very fast, towards her. As it shot by without changing speed she yelled after it in disgust and was actually stamping her foot in frustration and anger when the brake lights came on and the car shuddered to a halt. It began to reverse, quickly and accurately, stopping a few yards ahead of the Morgan.

Agnes ran down the bank, skirt flapping round her legs, and she stood, panting slightly, with one hand resting on the roof of the Morgan. It was then that she suddenly realised just how vulnerable she was, stuck here, on her own.

The white shape was now recognisable as a Jaguar XJS. Its owner unfolded himself from the interior and she gave him the once-over, trying to do a lightning summing up. All the warnings she had ever been given came flooding back and she furtively reached in and grabbed a spanner that was in the door pocket and concealed it in the large pocket of her skirt.

He didn't look like a homicidal maniac, or a rapist. He looked like a man in a hurry whose better nature had demanded that he stop. As he approached, the first spots of rain began to fall.

Frowning, he asked abruptly, 'Do you need help? What's wrong?'

The accent was transatlantic with only the faintest edge of politeness skimming the surface. Here was no chivalrous Don Quixote, eager to help a damsel in distress. The fact that Agnes hated playing the part of the damsel made her react more strongly than was politic.

'Oh, no, I usually do my daily exercises out here,' she replied, with honey sweetness, 'it's tremendously invigorating, and if I knew what was wrong I wouldn't be stranded, would I?'

A dark brow winged upwards and his eyes took her in properly for the first time. He lifted his hands and spread the fingers expressively, saying,

'OK, silly question. What actually happened?'

'It just petered out for no apparent reason.' She paused and added bluntly, 'Are you any good with engines?' The Morgan was her pride and joy.

'Some,' came the laconic reply. His gaze went over the gleaming yellow paintwork, and, walking to the front of the car, he placed his fingers on the handle, and went on crisply, 'Let's have the hood up, shall we?' and action followed the words.

Hood, meaning bonnet. Was he an American, Agnes wondered? She watched him go through the same check-list that she had used and realised he knew what he was doing and wasn't some crank pretending to be an expert. Once or twice his eyes lifted to her and then went back to scrutinising the engine, but there was a cool detachment in their depths that was reassuring.

I bet he thinks I'm a giddy, dumb blonde, Agnes thought, having long ago come to terms with this attitude but now and again allowing a niggle of annoyance some life. She knew that her hair would be getting frizzier every second with the rain and her twenty-seven years had probably been assessed reprehensibly younger. However, so long as he got the Morgan going, he could think what he liked.

'Not much wrong here, from what I can see,' he observed, still staring down at the engine.

'Why, that's exactly what I thought,' Agnes said with beautiful lack of expression.

His head came up and she outstared him, knowing she was being unreasonable, but some devil inside her egging her on.

'You know something about engines?' he asked, his words a soft drawl.

'Some,' she replied as laconically as he had, mere seconds ago. She thought she had pierced his detachment slightly but he made no reply, straightening, and studying his oil-streaked hands. He went to take out a crisp white handkerchief from the top pocket of his immaculate houndstooth check suit which now had rain pattern added to its surface.

'Hold it,' Agnes exclaimed, eyeing the suit. 'It looks as if I'm going to have enough on my conscience without you ruining handkerchief as well as suit. Use this,' and she dived her head inside the Morgan and brought out a length of paper towelling. She handed it to him and went on, 'Look, this is silly. You're going to get wet— we're both going to get wet, and maybe all for nothing. Why don't you give me a lift to the next garage? It's not far and——'

'Try starting it again.'

He was a dab hand at giving orders, Agnes decided, biting her lip and holding her tongue with difficulty. A 'do this, do that', sort of bloke. She was in no position to point out that a please and thank you now and again softened the impact. And his suit and his health were now definitely his own affair. She had given him the opportunity to get under cover before he was absolutely soaked to the skin and he had refused. . .so it was up to him from here on. As she slid behind the wheel to do as she was bidden, she muttered to the Morgan under her breath, 'If you start now, I'll never forgive you,' which she knew was bizarre, as the whole point of the exercise was to get the dratted thing moving.

Through the rain-splattered windscreen she saw him lift his head and give her a nod as a signal and she turned the key, and again twice more, and when nothing happened he came round and stood with his hands on the soft top, staring down at the dashboard as if the answer was there.

He doesn't like to be beaten, thought Agnes with unfair satisfaction, as she regarded his puckered brow and compressed lips. Now why, for heaven's sake, did that make her feel good? There was something about this man that both attracted and needled her and these two ambivalent feelings were odd and uncomfortable. She resolved firmly to be more amenable.

'This isn't a very clever situation to be in,' he said suddenly, his tone abrupt and censorious as his gaze transferred from the dashboard to her face.

Hackles rising, newly made resolve dying rapidly, 'Well, naturally,' Agnes agreed, as if talking to an idiot. 'Cars are meant to move and——'

'I'm not talking about the car, I'm talking about you being on your own, out here, miles from anywhere, and stopping a stranger for help. I could be anyone.'

'Well, you're not,' she replied shortly, cheeks spotted with colour. It didn't help that he was making a valid point but, really, he was treating her like an irresponsible teenager.

'I agree, I'm not, but you didn't know that.'

'Of course I didn't, I was taking a chance. What was I expected to do, for God's sake. . .let you go by? Wait until someone I knew came along? Be stuck here all night? I do realise the danger. You've made your point. In future I'll make sure I break down in the centre of town!'

He made no reply to this piece of nonsense and left her, walking back to the engine.

Agnes let out a long, steadying breath, banking down her indignation. Of course this wasn't the ideal situation to be in—any idiot would know that! The spanner felt heavy against her thigh and she brought it from her pocket and dropped it back into the door pouch, sensing that as a defence weapon it wouldn't impress him much. She gazed out front, and, for something to do, began to study him, trying for a degree of impartiality.

He was, she judged, over six feet tall, lean, with one of those faces that gave meaning to the word 'inscrutable'. His dark brown hair was taking a battering by the strong gusts of wind; it was thick, straight and well cut. There were deep lines scored either side of a rather cynical mouth, so it was possible that he eased up on the more serious side of life now and then and cracked his face with a smile, and she made a guess that his eyes were grey. He was quite attractive, she conceded, in a sort of sardonic way, but not her type. There was something about him that made her feel contrary.

He glanced up and caught her staring and there was that in his look that made her reassess her thoughts—he might have the capacity to rub her up the wrong way, but he also aroused a certain amount of interest and curiosity in her.

She came to a decision and flung open the door, thrusting herself out, saying firmly, 'I can't possibly take up any more of your time. I think it would be more practical to leave the car here and for you to give me a lift to the garage.' She stopped speaking as it was obvious that he wasn't taking any notice. He stood impervious to the weather, gazing into the distant hills, and she could almost see his brain ticking over, rejecting each possibility as it came to him.

He likes to see a thing through to the bitter end, Agnes judged, suddenly warming to this aspect of his make-up. She could identify with this quirk of personality, for she possessed it herself. However, enough was enough, and he needed the Morgan and its problem the way he needed a pain in the neck.

'Shall we go, then?' she prompted, and his head swung round, an arrested look on his face and there was weary foreboding in his voice as he asked with painstaking diction, 'You do, I trust, have gas in the tank?'

Eyes widening and all sympathy disappearing, Agnes said coldly, 'I might look an idiot, but I assure you I can read the petrol gauge as well as the next man.'

He studied her glacial stare for a few seconds and replied with a pronounced drawl, 'An idiot you surely do not look, but even the next man can make a mistake.' He opened the driver's door, glancing up at the sky, adding, 'Get in, there's no need for us both to get soaked.'

She stayed right where she was. 'Has anyone ever told you that you're exceedingly bossy?'

'Frequently. Has anyone ever told you that you're stubborn?'

Giving him a speaking look, Agnes obliged. Her skirt was revoltingly damp against her legs and rain was trickling down the neck of her shirt but she was damned if she would let him see how uncomfortable she was. She would be as stoical as he.

He reached in and turned the ignition and they watched the needle creep up to just below the halfway mark. Agnes turned her face and gave him a polite smile, which she thought probably ended up more of a satisfied smirk. Leaning with an elbow on the soft top rim, the other arm straight, hand clasped round his knee, bending slightly, he held her look calmly, and his eyes were grey, she found, quite the clearest grey she had ever seen.

'Where I come from,' he commented mildly, 'it can be dangerous to rely too heavily on gadgets; the old brain box needs to be ticking over all the time.'

'Really?' Curiosity got the better of her. 'And where's that?'

'Canada.' He eyed her thoughtfully. 'How many miles have you done since you filled up the tank?'

This was the moment when it would have been helpful for the earth to open and swallow the Morgan and herself completely as she took in the implication of the question.

Features incredibly controlled, he added encouragingly, 'Mmm? Miles per gas consumption——'

'I know what you mean, for heaven's sake!' burst out Agnes, glaring, doing frantic sums in her head. 'It is possible,' she said finally, colour high, 'that I'm out of petrol.'

There was silence while the only sound was the rain on the soft top.

'I see.' His tone was wonderfully level and not a muscle moved on his face. 'Then maybe we'd better check?'

'Maybe we had,' she replied heavily, and, as he made to move away, she added under her breath, 'and this is where I die of embarrassment.'

'I doubt that. You seem capable of talking yourself out of anything. The keys, please, to unlock the gas cap.' His hand came through the window opening and in silence Agnes handed over the key ring and he moved out of sight.

She waited, biting her bottom lip, hoping against hope that he was wrong. Running out of petrol! She gave a groaning sigh. The simplest and first thing one should think of when a car stopped without warning. Why, oh, why, hadn't she thought of checking the mileage and then she would have realised that the gauge wasn't working!

She heard him call, 'Hold on,' and then the Morgan was violently shaken from side to side. After a moment he reappeared at the window and handed her the keys. She switched on and, with two pairs of eyes fixed on the dial, the needle stayed where it was on empty.

Into the ensuing silence he drawled, 'Well, I guess we now know what's wrong.'

What a rotten trick to happen, groaned Agnes inwardly, glaring at the gauge, willing it to rise and knowing it was in vain. Obviously the wretched float in the tank was faulty and jolting the Morgan had freed it. Not much good showing empty *now*, she fumed.

She took a deep breath and said, 'Thank you for finding out the trouble.' She stared out front.

A flicker of amusement crossed his face. 'Being proved an idiot can be galling,' he agreed, and Agnes swung round, amber eyes locking with twinkling grey ones. She burst out laughing.

'I give you full permission to say what you like,' she declared. 'I'm furious with myself—how could I be so stupid?'

'No, no, it can happen to anyone.'

She eyed him sceptically. 'I bet it hasn't to you.'

'It has, and in much worse conditions, I promise you. I guess you have to do it once before you get into the habit of checking things for yourself.'

'It's noble of you to tell me.' Agnes gave an expressive shrug of the shoulders. 'Well, that's that. If you can give me a lift to the next garage I'll get someone to bring me back with a can.'

He straightened, saying, 'There's no need. I have one with me.'

Disgust was in her voice. 'How revoltingly far-sighted of you. I bet you've even brought food along with you,' and her tone was heavy with gloom. 'Are you always as organised as this?' she demanded. 'It must be terribly hard to live up to.'

'So my family tells me,' he drawled, giving a slow, lazy smile which totally transformed his lean cynical features before he moved off to his car.

'Wow!' breathed Agnes, jolted beyond reason. That smile was quite something! Rare but not extinct. And although he must be relieved to have found out what was wrong with the Morgan, he hadn't over-played his hand when it turned out to be something she should have cottoned on to earlier. She watched him lift up the boot and delve inside the XJS. The rain, she noticed ruefully, had stopped, but much too late to save his suit, although being drenched didn't seem to be bothering him. Luckily the tempera-ture was still fairly high and though they were

damp they were not cold. He walked towards the
Morgan, carrying the can of petrol, and as he
passed by the window he dropped something
into her lap. It was a rosy red apple. She gave a
smile, rubbed it on her sweater and took a bite.
Half of it was eaten by the time he was back at
the window, saying, 'Try it now and let's see if
that's done the trick.'

Agnes nodded. After a couple of attempts the
engine caught and fired and she cried, 'Eureka!'
and turned a delighted face his way, saying
warmly, 'That's great! I really am truly
grateful. . .'

'Forget it,' he said dismissively. 'Just remember
to renew the gauge as soon as you can.'

'You bet I will,' she responded wryly, and
reached for her purse, adding, 'I must pay you for
the petrol.'

'My pleasure.'

She stared up at him, nonplussed. 'I can't let
you do that,' she argued and again that mobile
eyebrow tweaked upwards.

'Why not?'

'Well, because. . .' For once Agnes was at a loss
for words. 'Because I don't know you. I mean,
we're strangers. . .'

'That's soon rectified. Alexander Brandon.' His
hand came through the window and hers came
up to meet it with a will of its own.

'Agnes Quinn,' she replied, and then rallied as
she went on firmly, 'Even so, Mr Brandon, I see

no reason why you should be out of pocket on my account. I'm deeply enough in your debt without owing you money as well. I really would like to pay.' This was as far as she could take it. Haggling over a gallon of petrol was a little undignified but the wretched man was making her feel guilty. He had no business to turn out human after all, although, even now, there was still something inexorable about him that made her want to push to the limits.

'I know you would.' His voice was dry, the sardonic features amused. 'I suspect you're an independent lady, Miss Quinn, but now and again you must allow us poor males the illusion that chivalry is not totally dead. It lifts our morale and makes us feel good. Donate the money to your favourite charity if it bothers you that much.' He tilted his head, listening with concentration to the sound of the engine. 'She seems to be running smoothly.' He stroked the paintwork, adding, 'I admire your choice of motor. Have you far to go now?'

Agnes dropped her purse into the holdall, knowing when she was beaten. Any more protests would be churlish and she hadn't behaved too well as it was. 'I'm making for Glen Rhu,' she told him. 'Do you know it?'

He nodded to show that he did and said, 'I'll drive behind you for a few miles. To be on the safe side.'

Agnes opened her mouth to protest and shut it

again, knowing by the gleam in his eye that she would be wasting her breath.

'Goodbye, Mr Brandon,' she said instead. 'Thank you for stopping, for your help, for the petrol and for the apple.' She held up the half-eaten fruit.

'Glad I've been of use.' He studied her, head tilted a little, the faint lines round his mouth creasing almost, but not quite, into a smile. 'Does anyone call you Aggie?' he asked.

A flash flood of mixed emotions swept through her.

'It's a brave man who tries,' Agnes said.

His brows rose. 'Not even in exceptional circumstances?' There was a definitely amused light in his eyes.

'Never,' said Agnes firmly, dousing the slight heat that had come to her cheeks. 'No one *ever* calls me Aggie.'

'Pity.' The smile deepened; he gave the smallest inclination of his head and moved away, his 'Goodbye, Miss Quinn,' floating back to her. At the door of his car he turned and raised his hand in a salute before getting in.

'Holy Grail,' intoned Agnes, feeling somewhat winded. 'For two pins I reckon he'd have tried.' She blew out a breath and then gave a laugh. 'What a ninny! Blushing like that!' She wrinkled her nose thoughtfully.

The engine of the XJS sprung to life. She engaged gear and drove slowly past it, her eyes

going to the mirror to see that it had moved up
behind her. She concentrated on the wet road and
the bends—she had no intention of disgracing
herself further by skidding off the mountain.

Now and then she checked the mirror and the
white car remained in view a safe distance away.
A splatter of rain hit the windscreen and she set
the wipers going. She should have offered to pay
for his suit to be cleaned and pressed, she thought
suddenly. Not that he would have let her. She
gave a shrug. What the heck.

Aggie. . . Huh! Though he did manage to make
it sound amazingly attractive with his Canadian
drawl.

Alexander. Was he called Alex, she wondered?
Odd. It was a long time since any man had
aroused in her such a welter of confused feelings,
most of them diametrically opposed! If they had
met, say, round a dinner table, then it might have
been fun finding out what made him tick.

At a place where the road widened, the XJS
swept by, accompanied by a succession of short
toots on the horn. Agnes waved in reply and soon
the tail lights were disappearing rapidly in the
distance.

'That's that, then,' she said, thinking; I wish I'd
asked more when I had the chance. Canada, for
one. Where and when and what. She pulled a face
and took a bite of the apple, relegating Alexander
Brandon to the store of amusing tales to be told

against herself, and at last came to the Ardneath turn-off.

Fifteen minutes later Cluny Cottage came into view and all she could think of was food, a hot drink and sleep, in that order. Tall Canadians with deep voices were forgotten.

CHAPTER TWO

AGNES woke the next morning to clear blue skies. She lay in bed, enjoying being back at the cottage in the small quaint loft room. She threw back the covers and went to the window, pushing it open and leaning out. She took a deep breath and expelled it noisily, feeling for the first time in weeks at peace with the world.

The picture before her was one she remembered when life in the city became too hectic, and she loved it deeply. Ahead was the small front garden of Cluny Cottage with its white wooden fence and gate and profusion of hardy shrubs and flowers. Beyond was the dirt road and meadow grass sloping down to the river. Across the river, half-way up the hillside, was the McFinlay croft.

Agnes smiled as she thought of Hector and Kirsten McFinlay. They were dears and spoiled her dreadfully. She had arrived to a welcoming fire in the grate—although one wasn't really necessary—and the evocative smell of peat, must and beeswax hit her as she stepped inside the cottage. A basket stood on the table, covered by a white cloth, and inside were Kirsten's delicious oatcakes, wholemeal rolls and fresh milk and butter produced on the croft. Agnes had eaten hungrily, gone to bed and slept like a log, and now she was ready for anything.

She leaned further out of the window and swung her head to the left where the river disappeared behind trees. At that western end of Glen Rhu the countryside was rocky and harsh, with the Ard River running swiftly through deep gorges, rushing and tumbling angrily over huge boulders dropped as if by giants' hands into the river bed. As the river flowed eastwards it became less fierce and the land became softer until it emptied its waters into Loch Rhu.

Agnes withdrew from the window and saw by the clock that it was nearly seven o'clock and knew she couldn't put off her first-day ritual any longer. Over her head came the striped nightshirt and on went a green towelling tracksuit. Pushing canvas slip-ons on her feet and taking a towel in her hand, she ran down the stairs and opened the back door.

She stood for a moment savouring the peace and tranquillity. A bird was singing in the old crab-apple tree in the orchard and a butterfly darted by in a flutter of colour. It was going to be a warm day, Agnes decided, and made her way up the hillside, brushing aside undergrowth and overhanging greenery as she followed the steep path.

Halfway up she branched off and soon could hear the noise of falling water, which became louder with every step, until she finally broke through into a clearing full of early morning sunshine. Light, catching the spray from the waterfall as it hit the pool below, turned the droplets into silver beads.

Agnes knew from past experience that it was senseless to hold back. The water was going to be freezing and no amount of hesitation was going to alter that fact. She stripped off the tracksuit in two swift movements, took a deep breath and plunged into the pool, giving a yelp of agonised laughter. She sank totally beneath the surface, wondering if her poor body would ever recover, and came up for air, spluttering. She waded through the pool until she was able to stand on a rock under the fall. The water was invigorating and stung her body, making her skin glow, and when she had had enough she stepped out from under the cascade, feeling wonderfully alive. She smoothed back the hair from her face and as the water cleared from her eyes she froze, all movement suspended, as she met the tranquil gaze of the man who was standing on the opposite bank.

She stood transfixed for some seconds and then, with an indignant yell, sank down into the pool feeling astonishment, embarrassment and outrage in about that order.

'*What* the *hell*,' she demanded furiously, 'are you doing here?'

'I'm cooking breakfast,' said Alex Brandon.

Clenching her teeth to stop them chattering,

Agnes managed, 'Really? I don't see any break-fast,' allowing the tone of her voice to show all her feeling.

'It's going on nicely back there. Can I offer you some? There's plenty.' He paused. 'You know, I shouldn't stay in there much longer or you'll be a block of ice.' His voice was infuriatingly matter-of-fact. 'I presume you were just about to get out?'

'I was, and I shall,' Agnes ground out, 'when you have turned your back.'

'Surely,' Brandon agreed. 'Although modesty is a little late in the day, isn't it?' and a flicker of amusement showed in his face.

'*Will* you turn round?' she yelled, glaring, and waited as he did so, climbing quickly and awk-wardly from the water to the bank, shivering violently. 'No one comes here at this time,' she accused, towelling herself down furiously while keeping an eye on him in case he defaulted, 'and you're trespassing.'

'Am I?'

'Yes, you are. This is Cameron land.'

'Ah.'

'Is that all you can say?' she demanded crushingly.

'Well, I guess I could say that I've leased the Dower House.'

Agnes stopped drying herself, momentarily taken aback by this surprising bit of news. 'Oh.' She began to rub again, recovering her indig-nation. 'You could have had the decency to make yourself scarce.' She added strength to her voice. 'Couldn't you?'

'My dear girl, there wasn't time,' Brandon explained mildly. 'There I was, with the place to myself, minding my own business which happened to be getting rid of fish scales from my hands. I was drinking in the idyllic scene when a green wood nymph burst through the undergrowth and before I could say or do anything had stripped off in two seconds flat and leaped into the water. I was mesmerised.'

'Like hell you were—and I'm not finished yet,' Agnes warned as he made to turn round. 'What was the matter with your legs?' she went on witheringly. 'Paralysed?' She began to pull on the tracksuit, muttering with subdued violence under her breath as the arms and legs seemed to have a life of their own.

'The path,' Brandon explained patiently, 'was right by you.' He shrugged. 'You would have seen me creeping away. I thought the best policy was to stay where I was.'

'And you said *I* could talk myself out of anything,' Agnes commented crushingly. 'You can turn round now.'

'Thanks—it's difficult talking through the back of one's head.' He turned slowly and stood, relaxed and composed and with that detached air about him that was both reassuring and infuriating.

'I still say you had a nerve.' Agnes stared

balefully at him, thrusting one foot at a time into the slip-ons. 'A *gentleman* would have looked the other way.'

'Sure, but I'm a guy from the backwoods, ma'am,' Brandon offered with a hugely exaggerated drawl, 'and no way a gentleman. I guess those fellows miss out on all the best treats.' Not a muscle moved in his face as he made this outrageous statement.

Agnes clenched her jaw and hardened her heart, refusing to be seduced by his charm too soon. She said challengingly, 'You played the gentleman yesterday.'

'I can act the part when necessary, and we didn't know each other then.'

'We don't now,' she said, and felt a blush creep to her cheeks as that was not true in his case. He knew her very well now, thank you very much!

'All the more reason for you to join me at breakfast so we can rectify that. The trout should be cooked by now. Don't you fancy freshly caught trout cooked over an open fire and eaten in the wholesome fresh air?' He raised a brow encouragingly.

'That's too good an offer to miss,' Agnes said at last, having held his look for just the right amount of time.

'Good. Sitting on one's high horse can be pretty boring after a time. I'm glad you've climbed down,' and he held out a hand to help her across the stepping stones to his side of the water.

For two pins, Agnes thought darkly, she'd tell him what to do with his breakfast, and by the look of him, he knew it. However, she really was hungry—her mouth was watering merely at the thought of those trout—and her curiosity was aroused. When he had driven off yesterday she had thought their paths wouldn't cross again, and here he was. Chances handed out by fate should not be refused. She ignored his help, crossed nimbly over the stones and wondered what he was doing here at Ardneath.

As he led the way Agnes decided he was hardly recognisable as the man in the immaculate suit and swish car of yesterday. Everything he wore now looked as though it was an old and faithful friend, comfortable and well-washed. A sludge-coloured bushman's jacket was worn over faded khaki trousers and shirt. His shoes were of a stout walking type and he made his way through the wood like the backwoods man he reckoned he was. They broke into a natural dell where a fire was burning in a square of stones. Over this four trout, pierced by a twig, were suspended. The smell was out of this world and to Agnes's disgust her stomach rumbled loudly.

Alex Brandon gave her an amused look. 'Sit down and I'll do something about feeding you.' He indicated the stump of a fallen tree. As she came abreast of him his arm came out to stop her. 'Are you warm enough after your shower?' His voice was as free from personal involvement as that of a doctor with a patient. He touched her cheek. 'Hum, not as warm as you could be. What an Amazon you are.' He turned her to him and rubbed her arms and back until her colour satisifed him. 'That's better. Sit here in the sun and you'll do.'

Agnes did as she was told. Certainly the blood was coursing through her body much faster than it had been, but whether it was by reason of the invigorating rub-down, or because it had been given by someone who was beginning to arouse her interest more and more, she was not prepared to admit.

'You do like giving orders, don't you?' she told him mildly, rubbing her wet hair with the towel.

'Do I?' He seemed indifferent to the accusation, sitting on his haunches testing the fish with a stick.

'I hope you've had no ill effects from getting a soaking yesterday.' She sneaked looks at him through her hair and wondered what he did for a living. The two images of today and yesterday contrasted so much that it was difficult to assess him.

'None that I know of, up to now,' he replied, without looking up.

It was difficult not to notice that he looked fit enough. Taut strong muscles showed under the tightly stretched material of the trousers as he crouched, body poised and balanced on the balls of his feet. The flesh of his arms showing below the rolled up sleeves was tanned, as were his face and neck, indicating that here was no totally deskbound man.

'Do you bathe every day at the waterfall?' He glanced up as he put the question.

Agnes tossed her head, shaking her hair and running fingers through it in an effort to dry it more quickly. 'No, I'm not that mad,' she replied, laughing a little. 'It's something that started way back. A sort of dare with myself. I do have a shower rigged up at the cottage on the days I chicken out.' She shook back the hair from her face. 'Are they done?' she asked as he straightened from the fire.

'Uh-huh. . .you'll have to use your fingers, so be careful you don't burn yourself. If I'd known I was to entertain I'd have brought eating irons with me.' Brandon put two of the trout on a scrubbed flat stone and brought them over to her. 'I can, however, provide some wonderful home-baked bread by courtesy of a homely body called Kirsten.' He went to a knapsack lying on the grass and took out a round loaf from which he tore a hunk.

'I know Kirsten.'

'Do you?' He thought for a moment. 'Yes, of course you do. Here you are, ma'am. I even have a napkin. How's that for service?' and he handed her the bread wrapped in a clean white handkerchief.

'Is there no end to the man's ingenuity?' marvelled Agnes teasingly. 'Thank you.' She set to with enthusiasm. The fish was delicious, falling from the bone in tender pale flesh. The juice ran down her chin and she mopped it at with the bread. She glanced across and found Brandon watching her, a small smile on his face.

'I like to see a girl with an appetite,' he approved, holding back his head and dropping a chunk of fish into his mouth. 'It seems fashionable these days for females to peck at their food.'

'Trauma always makes me hungry,' came back Agnes darkly. 'Where did you catch these?'

'About half a mile down-river. There's a pool shaded by trees where someone has built a wooden landing stage.'

Agnes nodded. 'I know the place. I bet Hector McFinlay told you about it. He knows all the best spots.'

Brandon dropped a fish spine on to the fire and it sizzled loudly. 'Do you know the McFinlays well?' he asked.

Agnes grinned. 'Since I was six.'

'You don't sound a Scot.'

'I'm not, I'm English. We moved from the Midlands to Ardneath town. Then when I was sixteen my father was transferred again, but as I was at a crucial time in my education I became a school boarder and stayed with the Camerons at Ard House in the holidays.' She tossed her fishbone on to the fire. 'I must say, you can cook fish outdoors almost as well as Hector.'

'Praise indeed,' and Brandon gave a wide lazy smile.

'You're no stranger to living rough, Mr Brandon.'

'My paternal grandaddy was a lumberman and I used to spend vacations with him in the North. He taught me everything I know about living in the wilds. . .and don't you think you should call me Alex? After all, if we're both staying in the Glen we shall be bumping into each other, surely? As we've shared a few experiences together, formality seems a mite ridiculous, don't you think?' He indicated the fish. 'Sharing breakfast being one of them. Have you warmed up now?'

'Yes, thanks.' Agnes decided to ignore any of the other experiences he could name and concentrated on eating. The sun was warm on her back. The trout, as promised, had that extra something to it that came from being cooked in the open and ever since she had woken life seemed to be touched with a sense of unreality.

Except she could hardly call Alex Brandon unreal. He was very much solid flesh and much too intrusive for comfort. Everything seemed to be highlighted. The bushes, the trees, the stones round the campfire, even. Agnes seemed to be looking at herself as if from the outside. Her skin was alive and glowing, her hair felt light and buoyant, settling against her cheek or swinging on her shoulders almost in slow motion as she moved. The texture of the tracksuit felt unusual;

even how she was eating was special. And Alex
Brandon, sitting a few yards away, had a strong
physical and personal aura which attracted her
with a strength that was unnerving.

'Something troubling you, Agnes?'

Agnes jumped and realised she was frowning.
She could hardly say that he was the cause of her
expression, and she flapped a dismissive hand.
'You said you spent vacations in the North,' she
prompted. 'North of where?'

'British Columbia, sometimes the Yukon—often
into the Rockies. That's rough country, wild and
beautiful. . .a real test of endurance. But I was
born in Vancouver.' He gave a rueful shrug. 'By
that time we Brandons had become socially
inclined.' The smile he gave was a touch sardonic.
'I've always considered that to be a pity, but I
guess you can't halt progress. Like living in
houses instead of log cabins and marrying girls
from respectable families.' He gave a laugh. 'My
grandaddy never did conform and I loved those
vacations.'

'This fish is perfection,' Agnes avowed, 'but I
can't manage both. Do have my other one.'

Alex rose to his feet in one fluid movement and
leaned over to spear her fish. 'My grandaddy
always used to say, "Eat a good breakfast, son,
because you never know where the next meal may
come from," and he was speaking from some hair-
raising experiences.' He shook his head, remembering. 'He was a real character.'

'He sounds it.' Agnes liked the warmth showing in his voice. 'Is he still alive?'

'No. He knew he hadn't long to live and disappeared into the mountains and we never saw him again. He died the way he wanted, in the place he loved more than anywhere.' His mouth twisted into a grimace of a smile. 'Confused the law a little, but then, that was grandaddy's way. Always was cussed.' Alex gave a silent laugh and then eyed her thoughtfully. 'What did you do after boarding school?'

'I went to university, but I always kept in touch with the Camerons.'

'My landlords.' He took the remains of her breakfast and dropped them on to the fire.

'Mine too, actually. Lord Cameron died earlier this year and his son, Stuart, is now laird. . .that's a courtesy title from way back. It doesn't mean much these days but the estate people still use it.' She glanced down at her hands and pulled a face. 'I think I'd better wash, or I'll be smelling of fish all day.'

'I'm sorry I can't offer you coffee, but that's outside my capabilities. Another time and I'll be more prepared.'

Agnes found herself saying, 'My cottage is only a few steps down the hill. I shall be making coffee if you want to join me.'

'That sounds an excellent idea.' His voice was reassuringly casual. If he'd sounded eager she would have instantly regretted the invitation. He scooped up earth and doused the fire, stamping it out firmly. Picking up rods and rucksack he gestured for her to lead the way and when they came to the waterfall they both stooped to wash their hands.

'Do you come to Scotland often?' Agnes asked as she offered him a share of the towel.

'When I can. The place has a pull. My paternal ancestors were Scots—they emigrated to Canada way back. They were very poor.' His mouth went down at the sides as if mocking himself. 'I like to believe that they know their descendants have made out OK.' He sprang across the stones and waited for her. 'Is your cottage the one near the bridge?'

'That's the one. It's very old.' She took the lead down the hill, concentrating on not getting entangled with branches until they broke out from the wood and the cottage lay before them in the sunlight. They passed through the orchard and walked up the path. Agnes pushed open the back door and they went in, Alex having to duck his head under the lintel.

'Sorry, I should have warned you,' she apologised. 'Everyone was so much smaller when this was built.'

'How many rooms has it?' Alex asked, looking round.

'Originally only two, the type they called a but-and-ben, but the loft has been converted into a bedroom and a wash place built on the side, with ingenious plumbing from the pool back there. Primitive but adequate.

While talking, Agnes had been pumping water at the sink and busying herself at the cupboards, collecting the coffee things. She glanced back to find Alex smoothing the palm of his hand along the surface of the dresser which held her crockery. He caught her look and said, 'Good, solid furniture with a clean, practical line to last quite a few lifetimes. This cottage may be primitive by today's standards,' he observed, his eyes going round the stone walls, the flagged floor, taking in the open hearth and the piled peat, 'but it's beautiful. I guess you must love it here.'

Agnes stilled, feeling a rush of pleasure at his words. 'I do,' she said simply, and gave him a warm smile. 'Now I'll put the coffee on and get changed.'

'Go ahead, don't worry about me,' her guest replied, making himself at home in an armchair.

I shan't do that, thought Agnes drily, as she climbed the steep curved stairs to her room and pulled off the tracksuit. Alex Brandon is perfectly capable of taking care of himself, she went on to reflect, as she donned jeans and a yellow T-shirt. Her hair was a lively, undisciplined mass about which she could do nothing in a hurry, so she abandoned it without a qualm. No way was she going to give the guy the idea that she was prettifying herself up for him. When she re-entered the kitchen a pungent smell of coffee filled the room.

Alex Brandon was leafing through a book which Agnes recognised as being a compilation of First World War poems. His choice interested her.

'How do you like your coffee?' she asked.

He murmured, 'Black, one sugar, please,' engrossed. She controlled a rueful smile. He couldn't be accused of overdoing the flattering attention, so she didn't need to worry about giving the wrong impression of herself! She poured the coffee and offered him a cup.

He now put aside the book as she asked. 'How long have you been at the Dower House?'

'Three weeks, on and off. I've had to go to Edinburgh a few times during that period. I was on my way back from there yesterday.'

'Edinburgh?' Agnes sat down on a wooden stool. 'Then we could have bumped into each other any time.'

'Could we?' His brows shot up. 'You live there?'

She nodded, taking a drink of coffee before explaining, 'I stayed on after university.'

'And what do you do in Edinburgh to earn the pennies?' His voice was lazily inquisitive.

'I'm a freelance designer—fabric and interior design.'

'Are you any good?'

'Yes.'

He smiled and she found she was smiling back, a silly, idiotic feeling of pleasure stealing through her.

What was it about some people that they could

pick up and tune into the same wavelength? There was, naturally, the old, old story of sex appeal, and Alex Brandon had his fair share, but this was something over and above that. With some people you wanted to dig deeper into their minds. Agnes suspected that if he gave you the chance this man would be worth exploring. . .the crucial words being, if he gave you the chance. He wouldn't offer anything of himself easily, and certainly not accidentally.

'And how do *you* "earn the pennies"?' she asked, pouring them both more coffee.

'I'm between jobs at the moment—I guess I have itchy feet.' He grinned. 'I've tried my hand at various things—lumberjack, waiter, mountain rescue, bellhop, bank clerk.' His mouth widened and he broke into laughter as if remembering. 'I'm refusing to think about work. I'm on holiday, enjoying myself.' He held up the book of poems. 'What do you think of these?'

For the next half-hour they discussed favourite authors and poets, the conversation broadening to theatre and art, until Alex said, 'This is very pleasant, but I must go. I'm expecting a phone call.' He unfolded his long body from the chair. 'Thanks for the coffee, and your company at breakfast. Perhaps we could do it again some time? By appointment, of course.' His face was now deadpan, but Agnes knew they were both recalling their impromptu encounter at the water-fall rather than the sharing of breakfast. She walked with him to the door, hardly knowing what she wanted—for him to stay so that they could carry on talking, or for him to go, so that she could assemble and digest all that had happened that morning. She stepped out on to the paving stones, feeling the heat of the sun strike her face. She plucked a head of lavender from the bush growing along the path and rubbed it between her fingers, her eyes sweeping the orchard contentedly.

'Goodbye, Agnes.' Alex picked up his rods and rucksack from where he had left them. 'I guess——'

'Oh, my God!'

He stopped, surprised by the heartfelt cry. 'What's wrong?' he asked, puzzled, following her dismayed look beyond the orchard.

'My bees!' she exclaimed dramatically. 'My bees are swarming and Hector's not here to help me!' She darted off, running swiftly through the orchard, stopping with caution at the edge of a small clearing. From one of two hives, bees were flying out in a thin line, zooming into the air in sweeping circles, volume gaining every second until they were whirling in a noisy joyous mass. Agnes watched in frustration, hands clenched, hopes dashed, a moan of disappointment bitten back.

'Can't we do what's necessary?' Alex had come up from behind to join her.

Agnes shook her head, an impatient denial on

her lips which died as she gave his suggestion more consideration. She turned an intent, piercing glance at him, weighing him up, and said, 'We just might—if you're game?'

'What are we waiting for?' came the laconic reply.

The light of challenge passed between them and she grinned, exhilaration radiating from her.

'Come on,' she rapped out, running back to the cottage. 'Here, fill this spray from the water butt,' and she pushed the spray and a bucket into his hands and darted into the cottage, coming out seconds later loaded with things in her arms.

'These are Hector's,' she said, handing Brandon a pair of gloves. 'And do up the buttons on your jacket, all of them.' She was putting on a long-sleeved jacket herself while talking, and, when buttoned up, pushed her hands into a similar pair of gloves.

As they walked quietly towards the hive she went on,

'What we want is for them to cluster somewhere convenient so I can lure them into the new hive. Will you spray them with water?' she whispered, and Alex Brandon, as he did as he was told, and keeping his voice as low as hers, asked,

'Why am I doing this?'

'I want them to think it's raining. They hate rain when they're swarming.'

Agnes stalked the bees crooning, 'Come on, my

lovelies—— Oh! Not on the tree, please! Yes, the gooseberry bush is terrific.'

Leaving him with instructions to spray them again if they looked like taking off, she hurried to open up the new hive. On her return she said softly, 'This is the tricky bit. The idea is to knock them into the basket——'

'There's one in your hair,' said Alex.

'Help! Is there? I should have covered up.'

'Stand still and I'll see what I can do.'

He took off the gloves and pushed them into his jacket pockets.

Agnes obeyed, and as he came close she was immediately aware of him as a man and not merely another pair of hands helping out during a tense operation.

As he gingerly lifted the strands of her hair in an effort to free the bee she raised her eyes cautiously to his face. It was a spare face, firmly defined. There was an old scar on his temple, his eyelashes had light brown tints as they fanned across his cheek and it was obvious he had set out that morning unshaven. This gave him a rakish, slightly disreputable air which, in an odd way, suited him and which Agnes, to her surprise, found amazingly attractive. And this was a guy who wasn't her type! Before she could analyse this face Alex's eyes lowered from her hair to her face and she found herself locked into a disturbing intent scrutiny, unable to look away.

'It seems determined to stay,' he observed

lazily. He glanced at the yellow T-shirt and then back to her hair. 'Perhaps it thinks you're a sunflower. Off you go, bee. There—it's away.'

Agnes waited for him to move away too, but he stayed where he was and everything within her alerted, panicked, and a confused jumble of signals shot in all directions before his head came down and his lips touched hers.

It was an astonishing coming together. The rightness of it so surprised her that she just stood there and accepted the kiss without a murmur, without any resistance. And why not? a brisk voice inside her head commented. It was a lovely day, life was good, they were both in a holiday mood, and what, for heaven's sake, was a kiss, after all? A kiss lightly, even a little cynically given, was to be received in a like manner. Just as she began to feel like responding, it was all over.

'As I thought,' Alex murmured, amusement in his voice. 'Sweet as honey.'

An ominous crescendo of buzzing saved Agnes from trying to find something flippant to say. She leaped into action, putting aside thoughts and feelings to be dealt with at a later date, and grabbed her end of the cloth she had brought. Alex took the other, and, with perfect timing, at a nodded signal, they toppled the bees, *en masse*, into the basket.

She carried it carefully to the new hive and transferred them into it without any problem. Giving a triumphant smile to her companion,

Agnes picked up a funnelled metal object and lit the contents with a match.

'This is, surprise, surprise, called a smoker,' she explained, puffing smoke round the hive. 'Bees hate fire and the smoke sends them into a panic of feeding. When they're full they feel contended and won't want to leave the hive. Simple but effective.' She stopped puffing the smoke and watched the hive closely.

'The basic needs—food and shelter,' offered Alex. 'What about that other basic need, love?'

Agnes grinned. 'Bees are extremely practical creatures. There's no sentiment in their make-up,' she said lightly. 'There, I think that should do the trick. We can leave them now.'

'Who looks after the hives when you're not here?' he asked, pulling off the gloves and rolling up his sleeves. They walked slowly back through the orchard.

'Hector, bless him, and we share the proceeds.' Agnes peeled off her own gloves and shot him a teasing side glance. 'You obey orders almost as well as you give them.'

He smiled at the dig. 'I'm glad I was around—it's been an interesting morning, in more ways then one.' He glanced at his watch.

She stopped in her tracks, groaning, 'Your telephone call! Have you missed it?'

'Probably.' He shrugged. 'She'll try again.'

My God, I bet she will! thought Agnes drily. 'I say, wait a minute,' she urged, and hurried indoors, returning seconds later carrying a jar. 'Here—try this and see what you think.'

'Thanks.' He took the jar of honey, placing it carefully into the rucksack. 'But you forget,' he went on with his lazy drawl, 'I've already had a taste, and it was delicious.' He stood looking at her, a ghost of a smile on his lips. 'Goodbye, Agnes. . . I guess I'll be seeing you around,' and then he was away down the path. At the corner he lifted a hand and was gone.

Agnes stared for some seconds at the empty space before going inside. The kitchen was refreshingly cool and shaded. She leaned on the sill and watched him make his way down the road, rods balanced on one shoulder, the strap of the bag over the other. His rangy leanness seemed to be more apparent from a distance.

She touched the tip of a finger to her lips and the feel of his mouth against hers returned vividly, together with the feelings he aroused.

'Oh, lor',' she mocked, brushing a wisp of hair from her eyes, 'anyone would think you've never been kissed before,' and she turned from the window and directed her thoughts to other things.

CHAPTER THREE

AGNES worked in the garden for the best part of the morning, also keeping her eye on her bees. The new tenant of the Dower House filled her thoughts with a persistence not easily dismissed. She sat back on her heels, a clump of weeds in her hand, remembering stepping out from under the waterfall, lifting her hands to her face and throwing back her hair. Then she had seen him and had frozen like a statue. Alexander Brandon would have had quite an eyeful, she reasoned darkly. So what? Irritably she stabbed the trowel with force into the earth. She wasn't ashamed of her body, although she liked to have control of where and when she showed it off—and to whom. Preferably not to a strange man one had met briefly only the day before.

The thought stopped her in her tracks. Yes, it was brief, but she was beginning to know certain expressions well. The mocking lifting of one brow; the slightly secretive smile; the swift gleam of amusement in the cool grey eyes; the guarded, almost sardonic set of his face in repose.

Yet he was still a stranger, and what the hell! Did it matter what he thought of her? She stilled. The question needed a truthful answer. Frowning, she searched inwardly. At the moment, no, it didn't, but she was honest enough to admit that, given any encouragement, it could matter. It all depended upon which part of her was the strongest—the bit that was attracted to him or the bit that jealously guarded her independence, and that meant her choice of lover as well as her life in general.

She checked the bees again and then went inside to change, swopping the T-shirt and jeans for a cool cotton dress and a sun hat. She left the cottage, leaving the key above the door in its usual place.

Agnes paused on the bridge and gazed down into the river, seeing her reflection dancing back at her. It was too bright for fishing now, she mused, and this thought conjured up an immediate picture of Alex Brandon, on his haunches, breaking off a hunk of bread. As the line of his throat and jaw impressed itself on her memory Agnes pushed from the rail and, startled, growled, 'For heaven's sake, woman, give the guy a rest, will you?' a little dismayed at the effect he was having on her.

She followed the track to the McFinlay croft. A lurcher bitch ran towards her, recognising her voice, and barking changed to profuse tail-wagging. Agnes bent down to give her some fuss, saying, 'Come on, Lass, let's go and find your mistress,' and, with Lass chasing circles round her, she ignored the front door and went round to the back. A woman in her early sixties was picking peas in the kitchen garden and she straightened and stared, eyes screwed up against the sun to see who it was.

'Kirsten,' called Agnes, 'it's me, Agnes,' and she made her way up the path between the vegetables. She gave the plump Kirsten McFinlay a hug, saying, 'I've come to thank you for the lovely goodies you baked for me; you're an angel.'

'Will you be minding my dirty hands on your clean dress,' Kirsten exclaimed, her words softened by the beam of pleasure on her face. 'Let me look at you, Agnes. Quiet, Lass, you daft animal!' Her eyes took in the smiling girl, with her sun-streaked hair and lightly tanned skin, and she went on, 'Och, you'll do, but you'd be far better off here in Ardneath than in any big city. Nasty air, Edinburgh.'

Agnes grinned. She knew well Kirsten's comments on big cities and Edinburgh in particular, knowing that the furthest Kirsten had ever travelled was to Inverness when she had broken an arm some years back.

'How are you, Kirsten?' she asked, realising with a pang of dismay that the years were finally beginning to show on her friend.

'Well enough. We both have the aching in the joints, but we're not grumbling.'

'It's good to see you again, and wonderful to be back. Isn't it an amazing day? I don't suppose Hector's around, is he?'

'No, he's away in the hills.' Kirsten picked up the trug of peas, prepared to abandon her job.

'Do you want to finish this row? Let me help,' offered Agnes and despite Kirsten's protests she began to pick the pods. 'Will you tell Hector that the bees swarmed this morning but that I managed to save them.'

'Did you, now?' Kirsten was suitably impressed.

'With help,' admitted Agnes quickly, wishing to be fair. 'The new tenant happened to be passing.'

'Aye,' responded Kirsten. 'Mr Brandon would be the helping kind, I'm thinking.'

Agnes was alerted. It would be interesting to find out Kirsten's opinion of this newcomer to the Glen. 'He waxed lyrical about your bread,' she offered as bait.

Kirsten shrugged as she added a couple of lettuces to the trug. 'He seems a pleasant gentleman. Hector is taken with him. Says he's canny with the rod, and, as you know, my man is not one easily pleased.'

Agnes knew this to be true. The tenants of the Dower House were a sensitive subject. As head keeper to the Cameron estate, Hector McFinlay's job was to be of service to the tenants and there had been many times when he had had to control his tongue—and sometimes failed—over some stupidity involving his beloved countryside. If he approved of Alex Brandon it was saying something.

'The Dower House is a bit big for him, isn't it?' observed Agnes, taking the trug from Kirsten.

'No, no, I think his family will be joining him for some of the time he is here.' Kirsten paused at a wooden seat and suggested, 'Shall we rest our legs for a wee while?' and she sat down heavily.

His family! Agnes felt a ridiculously acute sense of disappointment sweep over her and uttered a flat, 'Oh.'

'Aye, a brother has been spoken of.'

'Oh.' Agnes pulled herself together. She was beginning to look like a fish. She said lamely, 'That sort of a family,' and joined Kirsten on the seat. 'He could have had a wife and children.'

Kirsten shook her head. 'No, no. He was not speaking of a wife and children.'

So she hadn't received a kiss, however lightly given, that belonged to another woman.

'Though he must surely be of an age when he should be doing something about both,' Kirsten went on pointedly, adding, 'And the Laird too, I'm thinking.'

'Now, Kirsten, you know I've told you I'm not going to marry Stuart.'

'Aye, you have so, and a pity it is.'

Agnes didn't want to discuss the matter further. She glanced at her watch and made a muffled exclamation.

'Help! I should be on my way. Sorry, Kirsten, we'll chat another time.'

'Then you shall take eggs with you for the Big

House.' Kirsten rose to her feet, accepting a pull up from Agnes. 'If you call in on your way back there will be fresh milk for you.'

Agnes set off for Ard House, swinging the basket of eggs in one hand. Part of Ardneath's charm, she decided, lay in the old familiar patterns. How often had she taken eggs in a basket, like today, up to the Big House? It was like stepping into the past where everything was safe and uncomplicated, a place where adult worries and preoccupations could be shrugged off.

And yet not everything had been safe. Agnes suddenly shivered and her eyes swept the water. She focused on the Dower House nestling among the trees on the other side of the loch. The boat was missing from its moorings. Did that mean Alex Brandon was out in it? With narrowed eyes she searched the length of water that was visible but couldn't catch sight of a boat. Her gaze was drawn to the island. It looked so innocuous in the sunlight, a gentle, serene picture worthy of a calendar or postcard, with the backdrop of mountains and the blue-grey of the loch. Even the ruins on the island, blackened by fire and weathered by the elements over the years, seemed innocent of anything but being a heap of historic stones.

And so they are, she told herself with a self-mocking laugh. Hauntings and ghostly monks were childhood fantasies and as a repsonsible adult she didn't believe in such things—but she did believe in the power of the elements, and she shivered again as if icy fingers had touched her.

She turned away from the loch and passed through the park gates, walking up the drive to the house. Her step quickened. It would be good to see Jean again. Two years older than Agnes, Jean Cameron had lived at Ard House since she was a child. A distant relative, she had been taken in by the late Lord and Lady Cameron and brought up as their own. Jean had shared Agnes's childhood alongside that of her cousins, Stuart and Ian, and the two girls were close friends.

Ard House came into view. It was architecturally unworthy of note. Through the years alterations and additions had left the building oddly out of proportion, and, although Agnes recognised the validity of its being called ugly, she viewed it with loving, nostalgic eyes.

Mrs Minton, the housekeeper, showed Agnes into the Green Room where Jean Cameron was sitting.

'Hello, Jeannie, it seems ages since we saw each other,' greeted Agnes warmly. She bent down to give her friend a hug and a kiss. 'Here I am at last. Had you given me up? Did you get my letter? Kirsten sent these over,' and she held out the basket of eggs.

'Agnes, how lovely to see you.' Jean, small, a little plump and painfully shy with strangers, smiled, her face lighting up, and she touched Agnes's cheek with affection.

'Yes, your letter arrived—it is sweet of you to

write so often. Look Minty, brown eggs. Won't they be nice?'

Mrs Minton agreed, taking the basket from Agnes.

'Will I be making the coffee?'

'Yes, please, Minty, dear, and bring some of your wonderful griddle scones,' Jean answered sweetly. 'I'm sure we can tempt Agnes.'

Agnes groaned a laugh. 'Between you and Kirsten I shall go back pounds heavier!'

'Nonsense. Let me have a look at you,' Jean ordered gently smiling. 'How pretty you are, Agnes.'

Agnes grinned and sat down. 'You do wonders for my morale. Now, tell me all the news.'

'Stuart will be back any day now. I told him you had arrived when he rang yesterday to see how everything was. He said not to go back to Edinburgh before he came home or there'd be trouble. He'll be so pleased to see you, Agnes. He works hard, poor dear.' Jean paused and gave a small sigh. 'This house is much too big for us. It needs to be filled with children. . . Stuart's children.'

Agnes felt the blood steal into her cheeks but she made no effort to look away.

'I'm sure one day it will be,' she said quietly.

Jean was silent for a moment.

'How are your parents, Agnes?' she went on, throwing off the touch of sadness. 'Still liking New Zealand as much as ever?'

Agnes nodded. 'They're hoping to come over for a visit next year.' Her parents had eventually settled in New Zealand and were constantly giving hints that they would like her to join them.

'Stuart didn't mention that you were having a new tenant this year,' she went on, changing the subject.

'We were extremely lucky,' Jean replied. 'Our usual ones—you remember, the brewery syndicate—had to back out at the last moment. Our lawyer sent Mr Brandon to us. We liked each other and he had excellent references. He's Canadian and unmarried. Either he's adept at keeping his personal life to himself or else the local grapevine is slipping, for we know very little else about him.'

'Perhaps I can supply a few details.'

Jean sat upright, disbelief on her face.

'Agnes Quinn—do you mean to tell me you've met him?' she raised her eyes to the heavens. 'I can't believe it! Honestly, you only arrived last night!'

'We met on the journey,' Agnes said, chuckling, and went on to relate the petrol and bees incidents. She omitted their clash at the waterfall, not prepared to share that with anyone, not even Jean, aware that it would put a more intimate label on the relationship.

'He comes from British Columbia,' she offered nonchalantly, sipping her drink.

Jean shook her head wonderingly. 'I might have

known—you seem to attract unplanned happenings. I've only met him a few times, but I think I like him. He seems kind.'

Agnes made a strangled noise in her throat and Jean prodded with amused curiosity, 'Didn't you hit it off? Don't you think he's rather attractive in a sort of austere way?'

'If you like bossy, opinionated know-alls,' agreed Agnes, and Jean burst out laughing.

'What has he done to upset you?' she wondered. 'I wish I'd been there.'

'I'm merely reserving judgement on the man,' replied Agnes charitably.

They went on to talk of other things, catching up on general news and gossip until Agnes introduced a personal note.

'The thing is, Jean, I've reached a sort of crossroads. Anastasia is gradually becoming more well-known and the interior design side of the business is growing, which I'm pleased about as I like doing it. I've been lucky enough to attract one of the large paint manufacturers and they've commissioned some designs for curtains and wallpaper showing next year's shades.' She frowned. 'Unfortunately, I've got to move either now or when the lease runs out.'

'That's a shame,' sympathised Jean. 'You've made it lovely and it's so central.'

'I suppose that's why the place has shot up in value and been sold. It's being turned into business premises like most of the other buildings in the street. I guess it was inevitable, but I dislike someone breathing down my neck and waving money at me like this. It makes me contrary.' Agnes smiled wryly as Jean giggled. 'Anyway, I'm being pestered with solicitor's letters, which is one of the reasons for escaping here. It seems I'm the only tenant still holding out—the first-floor couple left last week. The offer is tempting in a monetary sense; they must want the building badly. So. . .do I look for a place which is bigger so that I can carry on working from home, which I like, or do I give in and find a small place to live and separate premises for Anastasia?' She wiped juice from her hands with a napkin. 'I'm supposed to be sorting all this out while I'm here.'

Jean said hesitantly, 'Have you thought that if, one day, you want to get married——?'

'I don't see why marriage should make a scrap of difference, Jeannie,' Agnes came back swiftly, 'not enough that something can't be worked out. I'll not stop designing totally; it's part of me, what I was trained to do. If I get married I don't see why I have to stop working, through if I have a family I'll obviously have to cut down.'

'What if your man wants you to stop?'

'He won't, or I wouldn't be anywhere near marrying him.'

As Agnes made preparations to go, Jean made a half-hearted protest.

'I'll be over again,' Agnes reassured her. 'I hope Stuart will give you time off from the estate's accounts and everything else you do while I'm here.'

'If you can't persuade him, no one else can,' Jean said teasingly. She shot her friend a glance, seemed about to ask something and then decided against it.

Agnes was glad that Jean hadn't asked about Stuart and herself. She knew Jean couldn't understand why she was holding back and she found it difficult to put it into words that wouldn't sound ridiculously idealistic.

Jean's gaze went beyond Agnes. 'Oh, dear. We have a visitor.'

Agnes swung round and directed her attention through the open window, following her friend's gaze. A man was coming through the garden. She saw him pause as if studying the house and then he continued on up the steps to the terrace.

As he hesitated at the window, Jean called, 'Come in, Mr Brandon. How kind of you to call.'

He stepped inside saying, 'Do forgive me, Miss Cameron, for coming this way, but I couldn't make anyone hear at the front.'

Jean lifted her hands expressively. 'Minton must be in the garage seeing to the car. Don't give it another thought. I believe you know Agnes Quinn, a very dear friend of ours.'

Formal acknowledgements were exchanged. Agnes saw that he too had changed his clothes and the cream shirt and light-coloured trousers were, to her experienced eye, expensive, well tailored in a high quality material. Yet he wore them with an air of one who had reached into his wardrobe without troubling himself overmuch at what came out—which scored points in his favour, Agnes decided. She liked men to take some interest in what they wore, but not obsessively so. She also noticed that he had found time to have a shave. He seemed far less approachable now than earlier.

'Mr Brandon—Alex—tell us what we may do for you,' Jean urged in her timid but kindly way.

'The telephone is out of order at the Dower House and I was wondering if it's still working here?'

Jean gave a soft exclamation of annoyance. 'How annoying for you. Agnes, would you be an angel and show Mr Brandon into Stuart's study?'

Agnes murmured, 'Yes, certainly,' and led the way out of the room. As they crossed the hall, for some reason she was more aware of her surroundings, seeing them through her companion's eyes—the portraits, the stags' heads, the huge trout in the glass case. She pushed open the study door and entered. This was one of her favourite rooms—wood panels and bookshelves and above the impressive fireplace a portrait in oils of a man in Highland dress. Seeing the Canadian's eyes drawn to it, she explained, 'That's the late Lord Cameron, Stuart's father.'

Alex Brandon studied it, offering, 'A very aristocratic-looking gentleman.'

Agnes pulled a wry face. 'He scared the hell out of me when I was a child,' she confessed.

Alex then turned to the other portrait in the room, one of Stuart Cameron on his twenty-first birthday, also wearing the tartan.

'Cameron doesn't take after his father,' he observed and Agnes agreed. 'Maybe that's just as well,' he added musingly.

'What do you mean?' she asked, on the defensive.

He turned his head and regarded her for a moment. 'I understand the late Laird fancied horses that came in last.' He took in the stony look on her face. 'I'm sorry—it seems to be common knowledge.' He paused and went on evenly, 'My lawyer told me.' He glanced back at the portraits. 'Not a happy legacy to leave one's son.'

Agnes felt the same but objected to this stranger to the glen criticising any of the Camerons. She lifted the telephone to her ear to check that it was working and handed it to him. At the door she asked, 'Do you think you can find your way back to the Green Room?'

With a hint of amusement in his voice, Alex said 'I guess so,' and she left the room.

Outside, Agnes stood still and composed herself. Damn the man, he certainly had the capacity to rile her. She hoped that he would lose his way, but doubted that would happen. No one could accuse Alex Brandon of being unobservant.

She suddenly felt the need to leave before he

came back but couldn't rush away too soon for politeness' sake. She had to wait until Brandon returned.

He entered the room saying, 'Thank you, Miss Cameron, I've left money on the table for the call.'

'You shouldn't have bothered.'

He offered her one of his exceptional smiles. 'Oh, I think so—Canada is hardly a local call. I've reported the fault on my line and hopefully they'll fix it.'

'You must use ours until they do,' pressed Jean. 'Won't you stay and have a sherry, or whatever you usually drink before lunch?'

'Thank you. Some other time, perhaps?'

'I'll hold you to that, Mr Brandon. Agnes, dear, it has been lovely to see you. I know Stuart will be over the moment he returns. Shall you go out by the garden?'

Agnes gave Jean a kiss, and, collecting her sun hat, followed Brandon out on to the terrace where they both turned to acknowledge their hostess before making their way down through the garden.

'A nice girl,' offered her companion.

'Yes,' agreed Agnes, donning her sun hat as they left the shelter of the trees. 'She's happy at Ard House. She and Stuart were brought up together.'

'Does young Cameron plan to marry?' A dark brow rose as Alex turned his head, searching her face. Fishing for information? Agnes determined not to satifsy him.

'Do I hear a cynical note in your voice, Mr Brandon?'

'You probably do.'

'You would advise Stuart against marrying, perhaps?'

'No. Why should you think that? I doubt he'd listen to me if his mind is made up.' He paused. 'Is it?'

'I have no idea,' lied Agnes. She had no intention of discussing her friends with a stranger.

'I thought you were going to call me Alex,' he said suddenly, stopping in his tracks, face turned to the sky as his eyes followed a hawk as it lazily circled above them.

'I've decided against it,' she came back tartly, 'in case you thought I was getting too familiar.'

'I'm not averse to familiarity—with the right person.' His eyes left the hawk and swung back to her, amusement in their depths. He studied her speculatively. 'And what are your views on the subject of marriage?'

'It may surprise you to learn that not all of us think that marrying is the prize at the end of the race,' Agnes told him with the hint of challenge in her eye.

'You reassure me,' he drawled.

She flapped her sun hat to create a breeze. 'We're just as capable of leading independent lives, and that's not to say I'm against marriage.

As an institution it has a lot going for it, but it's not on the top of my list for future achievements.' She eyed him keenly. 'You don't believe me, do you? Men, for some reason, seem to take it as a personal insult when a woman says that. I suppose to justify their feeling of superiority it's easier to disbelieve us.'

'Ouch! Some men may do,' Alex conceded. 'You don't believe then that women, generally, are monogamous creatures and are happier married?'

'That's a male myth,' Agnes said kindly. 'However, the conditioning of females from birth that their expectations in life must be one,' and here she counted out on her fingers, 'marriage, and, two, lower than men's, is changing fast. As long as we can keep a sense of proportion about it, we'll survive. We do, after all, need each other to preserve the human race.' She smiled at him, very sweetly.

Brandon inclined his head, an answering smile twitching his lips. They had reached the loch road by now and the Dower House boat was moored alongside the landing stage. Brandon strolled down the slope and on to the wooden planks and Agnes followed slowly.

'What is top of your list?' Alex quizzed, unhooking the rope from the post and stepping down easily into the boat.

Agnes brought her attention from the shimmering water, the blue sky and the green wooded hills and gave his question consideration.

'I don't think any one thing is,' she said at last. 'Quite a few things are important to me. Friendship, self-esteem, career achievement, a sense of adventure so that life doesn't become humdrum. When you have a couple of hours to spare, if you're interested, I'll develop the idea further. Of course, to a world-weary cynic like yourself, from the lofty age of. . .?' and she paused expectantly, raising her brows in question.

'Thirty-four.' The drawl was most pronounced, as was the amusement.

'Perhaps your list is different?'

He stopped what he was doing and studied her, an equally challenging expression in his eyes, although his answer was lazily given. 'No, not that much different, but you've left out something important.'

Agnes thought hard and then took the bait that was dangled, asking, 'What's that?'

'Passion.' The word came easily from his lips and he paused, taking her measure. 'I guess I was wondering if passion came under the heading of friendship or adventure,' and the smile that followed was slightly malevolent.

It was all very well playing verbal tennis with someone, but it was essential to keep your eye on the ball at the time. Alex Brandon had just served an ace.

Passion. Such an evocative word. Unbidden came the thought of lying in bed with him. She felt a frisson of longing sneak its way through her, and grinned inwardly. Oh-oh, Agnes, she mocked, you have enough problems as it is without adding Alexander Brandon to swell their numbers! A reply was obviously necessary so she said flippantly, 'Hopefully, both,' and turned to leave.

'Do you want a lift across?'

'Thanks, but no,' she threw over her shoulder. 'I'm calling in on Kirsten at the croft.'

She reached the top of the bank and swung round, watching him. About to push off, he glanced up and asked, 'What does Cameron think of your list of priorities?'

Agnes tensed. She felt like saying that she didn't know what he was getting at, but she disliked prevarication and couldn't bring herself to be evasive in front of that level stare.

'I haven't asked him,' she replied, voice level yet holding a definite note in it that should have warned him he was treading on dangerous ground. She might have known that it wouldn't put him off.

'He doesn't strike me as being the adventurous kind,' Alex reflected, tilting his head consideringly. 'A good enough, stolid type, no doubt, but a little lacking in imagination.'

Everything within her jolted. 'Really?' Her tone was heavily sarcastic. 'I wouldn't have thought you'd known him long enough to make a judgement.'

'Some don't take long.' He braced the oar against the post. 'I suppose the idea of being Lady

Cameron could be adventure enough for you.' He gave a push and the boat moved away from the landing stage. He sat down and pulled on the oars and the boat shot through the water, leaving a pattern of ripples in its wake.

Keeping a tight rein on her temper, Agnes called, 'Being part of all this,' and she flung out her arms, embracing the whole of the glen, '*and* a title? I should say so!' She turned and walked along the road, simmering with anger. How dared he insult her by insinuating that she could marry Stuart for his title? Bloody-minded moron! If he'd been standing next to her when he'd said it she would have knocked him in the loch with an inspired right hook!

CHAPTER FOUR

OVER the next few days Agnes alternated between bouts of laziness and bursts of energy. She helped Kirsten, joined Hector in overseeing the stock in the hills, took gentle walks with Jean and rode most mornings on a borrowed horse from Stuart's stables.

She had caught sight of Alexander Brandon in the distance once or twice during this time but did not come near enough to make contact. She hadn't made up her mind what she was going to say to him when she finally did. Each time she remembered his comment on the attractions of becoming the next Lady Cameron her blood boiled. And yet she was curious about him. There was something about the wretched man. . .

One afternoon she was walking along the eastern end of the loch on the way to a favourite childhood place where she intended to sit and puzzle out her future. She had passed the Dower House but had seen no signs of life; the boat was moored to its post and the XJS was parked by the house so she knew Alex Brandon was around somewhere and had not returned to Edinburgh.

She brought her thoughts back to leases and bank managers while following a rough track parallel to the water. It was not so warm but the day was fine enough to be wearing a vest-type T-shirt and a denim skirt cut to above the knee, plus a sweater slung round her shoulders in case she needed it.

So intent was she on her problems that she was almost upon Brandon before she saw him. He was standing a distance below, but still some way up from the shoreline, binoculars held to his eyes. She hesitated, unsure whether to pass on by, and at that moment he lowered the glasses and saw her. They stood, assessing each other with a certain amount of wariness on Agnes's part, and inscrutability on Alex's, and then he was motioning her to join him, putting a finger to his lips to indicate that she should be quiet.

Curiosity was ever her undoing. Agnes stepped off the track with commendable stealth and began to negotiate the uneven slope. A hidden tree root made her stumble. She recovered, overbalanced on a loose stone and then went flying downwards, legs and arms flailing. Her one thought was to make no noise and so her strangled yelp stayed in her throat. She heard a muttered exclamation from Alex, was aware that he threw himself in her path to try and save her and they were both rolling the remaining yards to where the slope levelled out into a hollow, the trunk of a tree stopping them from actually landing in the water.

When the world stopped spinning and air filled her lungs again Agnes found she was pinned to the ground. Her eyes, when she opened them, stared straight into grey ones, a droll gleam lurking in their depths.

'Oh, my God, I'm sorry,' she gasped, and took another deep breath.

'Be my guest,' Alex drawled, bringing one hand from under her and tweaking a leaf from her hair.

Now that the shock of the fall was beginning to recede, Agnes brought her attention to how she was feeling, thankful she was still in one piece after flexing her muscles. It was then that she became aware that her body was sending out violent messages to her brain, messages of a personal nature all to do with close bodily contact. She closed her eyes, worried that Alex might read too much from them and murmured, 'Don't you think we should get up?'

There was laughter in his voice. 'Why?' he asked. 'I'm rather enjoying myself, aren't you?' and she opened her eyes and found a teasing look on his face and definite messages in his eyes that made the blood course faster through her veins.

'I'm not at all sure I intend talking to you,' Agnes said with a burst of energy. 'That last time we spoke I distinctly remember feeling a strong inclination to wallop you one!'

'You don't consider that maybe you have?' His brows rose incredulously.

She bit her lip but couldn't stop her mouth from responding.

'And talking was not exactly what I had in

mind,' he went on, eyeing her lazily. He searched her face, taking his time, giving her the chance to resist if she wished. Agnes had no such wish. There was a feeling of inevitability about the whole thing. She could feel her heart thumping with extraordinary force and she was mesmerised by the shape and texture of his mouth.

The kiss began as a mere feather touch, a whimsical teasing, before his lips covered hers, whimsy gone.

Agnes melted totally, savouring the heady delight of being kissed with incredible rightness, an implosion of recognition shooting through her so that she responded instinctively. When the kiss finally ended she couldn't speak; she didn't seem to know whether she was on her head or her toes, what time of the day or year it was and how many beans made five. Inside her head the usual warnings were punch-drunk. Exultation and joy were neck and neck winners.

'I guess we can safely say we're both alive,' Alex murmured drawlingly, giving a dry small smile which was just a little lop-sided.

'And how!' gasped Agnes faintly. She stared up into his face still in a bemused fashion, trying to think rationally, but finding it hopeless when every inch of her was alive to the feel of him and the effect he was having on her. How was it possible? her intellect moaned, while her senses quivered and thrilled and leaped within her.

Alex carefully shifted his weight and lifted himself from her. He bent, holding out his hands and caught hers in a firm grasp, hauling her out of the hollow saying, 'Up you come.' Once she was on her feet he steadied her, gripping her by the shoulders, asking, 'Everything in working order?'

'Yes, I think so.' Agnes wriggled fingers and toes. 'A few bruises.' She turned to look at the slope of the hillside and swung back, addressing him ruefully with, 'I'm awfully sorry, Alex. Are you hurt?'

'Don't worry, I'm quite tough, and don't apologise. It's been worth it if only to hear you call me Alex,' and he smiled his slow, lazy smile.

Agnes found she was smiling back, her mouth outside her control stretched as wide as it could go, as if she had drunk vintage champagne. She wanted to laugh out loud as she remembered the confused mixture of feelings she had suffered each time they had met. This, then, was what all the songwriters were shouting about, all the poets, authors and ad men. And it had taken Agnes Anastasia Quinn twenty-seven years to find out what they meant!

Satisfied that she was steady on her feet, Alex stepped back a pace and began to free himself of dirt, leaves and other bits of vegetation he had collected on the way down.

Agnes was almost relieved when he let her go. As much as she thrilled to his touch, it was difficult to think straight and she needed to gather together some form of protective guard. She had, perhaps, already given too much away. She felt stunned, as if she had been knocked on the head—maybe she had? she reflected wryly, knowing it wasn't true. She followed suit and began to brush herself down and her surprised, 'Oh!' caught his attention.

They stared at the long scratch oozing blood from the shin of one of her legs.

'How funny. . .it's only beginning to hurt now I've found it,' Agnes observed, laughing a little.

Alex knelt, examining the wound closely. 'It doesn't look deep, but I think it ought to be bathed. There's a rill near here. Wait a moment.' He walked away, pushing through the undergrowth, returning some seconds later with a wet handkerchief.

'I seem to be making a habit of using your handkerchiefs one way or another,' she said, as he began to gently clean the wound. She looked down and felt the strongest impulse to put her hands on his head and run her fingers through his hair. He looked up suddenly, an alert expression on his face, and she wondered wildly if he could read her mind, because if he could she was completely lost.

'Did that hurt?'

She breathed a sigh of relief, smiled, and shook her head. 'I don't know what's happening to me this holiday. I can usually run my life quite efficiently. I reckon my planet and stars must be on a collision course. . .'

'Yes, with mine,' Alex finished drily. 'Does it feel OK?' he asked, rising, and Agnes said it felt fine. 'You must bathe it properly when you get back home, to be on the safe side.' He stood for a moment, regarding her thoughtfully, and then said, 'Stay right there,' and he left her, climbing back up the slope to where he had been standing before her impetuous arrival. Agnes saw him search the undergrowth and then return, carrying his binoculars. Scattering pine needles, he rejoined her, saying quietly, 'Let's see if our feathered friends are still here, or whether they were scared off by the noise.'

Agnes watched him, drinking in with hard-won objectiveness everything about him—the tousled dark hair, the strong profile, the tanned V of flesh exposed by the open shirt, the expanse of forearm, the long sensitive fingers clasping the glasses and the tall, wiry frame clad in the inevitable faded cottons.

What would it be like, she wondered, for those fingers to touch her where she liked to be touched? More than ever she knew he would be a good lover. Yet there was little of the lover about him at this minute. He had stepped back into his lazy, detached persona and her respect grew. There was nothing crude or excessive about Alex. Not many men knew when to leave well alone.

'Yes,' he murmured softly, 'they're still there.'

He reached out without turning and drew her in front of him, putting the glasses into her hand and guiding their direction. Speaking quietly, his breath warm on her cheek, he went on, 'Aim for that odd-shaped tree stump jutting out of the water then come down to the reeds.'

He was making no contact other than his hand over hers, and when she answered, 'Yes, I've got them,' his hand dropped instantly.

'What are they?' she asked. 'I don't think I've seen ducks of that type here before.'

'Pintails. They're quite rare. The male is the one with the chocolate-brown head and white vertical stripe. The female is the paler speckled one.'

'It's funny that in birds the female is always the dowdy one, isn't it?' She lowered the glasses and handed them back to him. 'I wonder if they'll stay and mate? I shall keep an eye open for them. We have a few pairs of grey heron nesting regularly.'

They began to make their way back up the hill. Pine needles and moss made the surface slippy and Alex, who had gone first, turned to help her to the path. As they walked slowly along, Agnes scanned the loch and the island. 'Have you been warned about the weather?' she asked suddenly. 'How it can change rapidly and be dangerous in the mountains or out on the loch if you're not prepared for it?'

'Cameron did mention something.' A nuance in her voice made Alex regard her more intently. 'Why do you ask?'

She didn't answer for a moment and then said, 'Stuart's twin brother Ian drowned in the loch.'

'Did he?' There was a pause while Alex digested this piece of information. 'When was this?'

'About ten years ago.' Agnes clasped her arms across her front as if she were cold. 'I was just turned seventeen, so Jean would have been nineteen and the boys nearly twenty-one.' It wasn't often she allowed herself to think too deeply about Ian.

'Tell me about it. Here, let's sit down.' Alex indicated a rough planked seat by the side of the road. The seat was a well chosen spot, giving an uninterrupted view of the water, with Ard House nestling behind trees on the far shore and the island with its ruins just off centre. Alex put one foot up on the seat, resting an elbow on knee, while Agnes sat down. She linked her hands round her knees.

'It was in October. We were fishing, the four of us, and it was a dull, misty day, just right for the fish to rise. We were having a good run of luck and I suppose that was why we weren't paying enough attention to the change in the sky, how much darker it was getting. Anyway, a squall blew up and before we knew it we were in difficulties. The boat was uncontrollable in the huge waves and wind.' She stopped.

'You don't have to go on if it upsets you,' Alex said quietly, and Agnes gave a little shake of the head, staring across the loch with a faraway look in her eyes.

'It's the waste,' she said pensively, 'and the guilt. Even after all this time.'

'Why should you feel guilty?'

She gave her shoulders a helpless lift. 'For being alive, I suppose.' She rubbed her bare arms up and down and then shrugged on the sweater, lifting her hair free and flipping it back. She went on matter-of-factly, 'It was rough and we were shipping water. When the boat finally capsized, throwing us all into the loch, we managed to cling on to it. After a while Ian decided to swim for the mainland to get help. He always took charge, it came naturally to him. Jean wasn't a strong swimmer and it was apparent she wouldn't be able to get very far in those conditions, and perhaps he thought we girls wouldn't be able to hang on for too long because of the cold and our wet clothes. I remember Stuart had an argument with him about who should go, and Ian told him he would, because he was the stronger swimmer and the eldest.' She gave a smile. 'He was, too. Good at games and born ten minutes before Stuart. They don't know what happened. Under normal conditions he could have swum the distance with no difficulty.'

'What happened to you three?'

'We were eventually driven on to the island by the gale and were picked up two hours later by Hector in the powered boat. Jean was ill with pneumonia afterwards and hasn't been on the loch since. Stuart rarely speaks of Ian.'

'And you?' Has it put you off going on the water?'

'It wasn't easy, but I knew I had to do it. I went with Hector the next day. We keep life-jackets in the boats now. I only told you because I understand you have your family coming to stay with you and I shouldn't like another accident to happen.' She embraced the view with both hands. 'It looks so calm and serene that it's necessary to know it can change its colours and be lethal.'

'Sure.' He gave a dry smile. 'And you already know my brother will visit,' and he shook his head in indulgent wonderment.

Agnes chuckled. 'The glen is a terrible place for gossip, like any enclosed community.' A movement in the sky attracted her attention and she asked idly, 'Is that a hawk?'

'Looks like a buzzard,' Alex answered, following the direction of her look. 'It has a shorter tail and darker markings than the hawk and the flight is more laboured too.' He passed her the glasses to have a closer look.

'Ah, yes, now I see.' She traced the buzzard's flight for a few seconds and then gave up. She glanced at Alex, enjoying this snippet, this facet, that could be built on to make up the whole of this man, and more and more she was becoming eager to know him. She handed back the glasses, saying, 'You certainly know your birds—and no pun intended,' she added, although she reckoned the same would apply to his women.

His mouth twitched as he replied with suspect gravity, 'If you're interested then your knowledge grows.'

'Yeah—I guess whatever you turned your mind to you'd make sure you could do it well,' Agnes came back with equal gravity.

'Friendship, adventure and passion,' Alex quoted, his voice embracing her, drawing her eyes to his face. She saw the corners of his mouth deepen and wondered how she could ever have thought it cynical. It was the most beautiful and sensitive mouth and she adored it. They stood, sizing each other up, and then the sound of a vehicle coming along the road stopped further talk. Agnes dragged her eyes from Alex's and he straightened but remained watching her, only turning when the Land Rover spurted dust as it halted level with them.

Agnes found, for the first time in her life, difficulty in meeting Stuart's smile with a purely spontaneous one of her own.

'Hello, there,' Stuart called through the open window, face beaming. He stopped the engine and jumped down. Crossing the space between them in a few swift strides, he hugged her and gave her a kiss, voicing a satisfied, 'Agnes—it's great to see you!' Still keeping an arm round her he stretched out a hand, saying, 'Good day, Brandon. I hope things are to your liking at Ardneath,' and

Alex's hand came up and they exchanged a brief but firm clasp. They began to discuss various things regarding Ardneath in particular and Scotland and Canada in general.

Agnes stood between them, not listening to the words but hearing the music of their voices. Stuart's was light and lilting, not noticeably Highland, but having the accented echoes of his ancestors in certain phrases and words. Alex's was deeper, more relaxed, with a lazy drawl. A flute and a cello, she decided with sudden poetic whimsy.

Physically they contrasted. Stuart was a thick-set, broad-chested man, a little over medium height, with light brown hair, blue eyes and a pleasant square-jawed face. He was dressed today as was usual on estate rounds in sweater, jodh-purs and riding boots, all broken in with continual wear.

Alex, by comparison, seemed taller, and, though his physique was hidden behind a mask of indolence at this moment, there was no mistak-ing the fitness and strength as he stood there, hands in trouser pockets, listening to Stuart.

Agnes wondered what he was thinking. It was impossible to guess for he was wearing his polite, disengaged face made more so by reason of Stuart's open, friendly one. As Alex's eyes flicked to her once, briefly, she felt she was coming under his cool scrutiny too; it gave her a prickly feeling and she was very conscious of Stuart's possessive arm round her shoulder.

'I've dropped a note into the Dower House,' Stuart was saying. 'I think it's about time we gave you a chance at a deer stalk. I've suggested to Hector two days hence and he's arranging things. If you say yes I'll give him the final go-ahead.'

'Thanks, I'm free then,' Alex said.

'Good. You'll come, Agnes, won't you? We'll make an early start. Pick you both up around six-thirty.' Stuart glanced at her. 'Come with me into Ardneath?'

Agnes smiled and nodded, thinking—this was Stuart, for heaven's sake, whom she hadn't seen in ages! Of course she was going with him.

Stuart opened the passenger door and she paused, looking across the bonnet at Alex, saying, 'Thanks for showing me the pintails.'

Alex inclined his head in silent acknowledgement and when Agnes looked back some yards down the road she saw he was no longer there.

CHAPTER FIVE

THE weather changed, bringing light rain and cool breezes. The morning of the deer stalk was dry, though misty.

Agnes woke before the alarm and lay in bed, thinking of Alex. This was an exercise she found she was drifting into frequently, thinking of Alex, and she closed her eyes and remembered everything about him—the kisses, his irresistible grey eyes, the way his hair grew, his hands, his smile. . . OK, OK, let's not think about him, she agreed with herself, groaning a laugh and thumping the pillow—at least, not the 'too too solid flesh' bit. Let's ponder the intangibles, like the teasing *badinage*, the sense of humour—so important—the couple of times he'd made her flaming mad—every relationship needed a pinch of pepper to it now and then—the intelligence, the depths to the man. She gave a deep, long drawn out sigh, smiling into the pillow. Everything added up to the fact that Alexander Brandon of Vancouver, British Columbia, Canada, had something extra special going for him. And how!

There was no denying that she was physically attracted to him—there was an incredible chemical reaction between them and the air positively sizzled round them, but she was not the type to commit herself to a relationship on mere passion alone. Agnes needed to be attracted by everything about a person, and that was usually the trouble— not many men lived up to her expectations.

She didn't feel that she was asking too much when she expected loyalty and trust and the right to be treated as a person with a mind and will of her own. She had reached the age of twenty-seven having fallen in love a few times and had suffered deep hurt in the process. Because she was attractive, vibrant, intelligent and amusing she didn't lack men friends, and gave freely of her spare time, enthusiasm and listening ability, but held back from any deeper relationship, not giving up on her ideal, but almost coming to the conclusion that he did not exist.

And then she had met Alex. . .and incredibly was very nearly at the point where she could throw caution to the wind. It was a heady thought and she had forgotten how wonderful and exhilarating falling in love was.

As for Alex himself—he was not a man to take incautious steps into anything, whether it was casting a fly for a wary trout in the river or enticing a female to forget all her previous disasters. . .with a 'no strings' clause to the contract. As Agnes began to get dressed she ruefully acknowledged that she could be likened to that trout. She was caught on the hook and with teasing care was being slowly eased to the bank.

There was, however, still enough time to decide whether to struggle free or let herself be caught.

When Stuart arrived, the Land Rover hurtling down the road to do a quick three-point turn, she hurried from the cottage and climbed in.

'Hi, Stuart,' she said, settling herself, and then, in some surprise, 'I thought Jean said she was coming?'

Stuart drove off, replying, 'She is, but she's gone with Hector to pick up Brandon and we're meeting them on Ardbeg.' He turned to give her a broad smile. 'This is just like old times, remember?'

Agnes returned the smile and nodded and they chatted for a while on a number of topics and Stuart suddenly said, 'I wonder if Brandon is up to taking Old Zeus?'

It was hardly a question that could be answered and Agnes did not attempt one. Old Zeus was their name for a stag, a true King of Beasts, who was showing his age these days, but who was still a wily creature. He had given good sport over the years and only the best stalkers ever came within range of him.

'After all, he has to be offered something worthwhile,' Stuart went on to observe a little gloomily.

Again Agnes remained silent. She sensed a certain amount of antagonism in Stuart towards Alex which she supposed was only natural. Usually the Dower House tenants were middle-aged and could be clearly placed. Alex Brandon, only three years old than Stuart, did not seem to fit into a clear category. Agnes didn't know whether Alex was capable of stalking a deer, or a good shot, but she remembered his grandaddy in the wilds of British Columbia, and guessed he could put up a competent enough showing.

She felt a certain measure of pride when she considered he was having such a chance at Ardneath. She had mixed feelings about the killing of birds and animals but she understood that it was necessary to maintain a healthy stock and that Ardneath was a wonderful sanctuary, a refuge, and not a preserve for the feeding up of game just for slaughter. It was to Stuart's credit that he did not abuse this, although he did have a responsibility to provide his tenants with whatever sporting activities they required.

'There's something odd about him,' Stuart announced.

Agnes replied cautiously, 'What do you mean, Stuart?'

He went on, 'Hector says he's a canny fisherman, but he isn't interested in the grouse. I did wonder about today. Whether he'd take me up on my offer.'

'That's not odd,' reasoned Agnes. 'Some people believe in killing only when it's a matter of survival. Maybe he's one of them.'

'Then why come to Ardneath and pay a pretty hefty sum for the privilege of missing out on the sport?' Stuart paused. 'What do you think of him, Agnes?'

'Mmm? Oh, he seems OK,' she answered casually, thinking, He's an infuriating, fascinating man and I'm as unsure of myself as if I were starting out on my first love-affair! Her eyes raked the landscape and saw that they were at the meeting place on Ardbeg mountain. Hector's green van was parked ahead and Hector himself, together with Jean and Alex, was standing by the side of it, drinking from a flask, the liquid sending steam into the chill early morning air. Some way off a couple of gillies, men from the estate who were helping with the stalk, stamped their feet and rubbed their hands.

'Sorry we're late,' Stuart called, pulling to a halt. Agnes climbed down and made her greetings. Alex moved to speak to the gillies and she noticed the easy way he engaged in talk with the two men.

'I thought something had happened to stop you from coming,' Jean exclaimed, tucking her arm through Agnes's. 'This is like old times, isn't it? Oh, Agnes, sometimes I miss Ian more, not less, as the years go by. Funny, isn't it?' This was given with quiet fervour and Agnes felt a sense of shock. Ian was so rarely spoken of between them. There was a brief poignant silence and then Jean said brightly, 'I say, Agnes, do you think Alex will get Old Zeus?' Her eyes went to Alex.

'He's foxed better men than Alex so far, Stuart

included, and could again,' Agnes replied. Alex chose that moment to look their way, and, excusing himself from the gillies, strolled over. Jean smiled at him and took his empty coffee-cup, leaving them to collect up the others.

'Is something the matter?' he asked, and under the steady scrutiny of those analytical grey eyes Agnes found herself feeling flustered.

Surely he couldn't have guessed how she felt about him? This man is too darned disconcerning, she thought, as she answered airily,

'Nothing that a good tramp in the mountains won't put right.'

Into the silence that followed Stuart came up, saying, 'Hector reckons this will lift later,' and he assessed the thick white mist that lay over the countryside. 'He's taking the van with the gillies to Ardmoor and will keep the glasses on the herd and encourage them our way if necessary.' He looked at each of them in turn and asked, 'Ready? Then we'll away.'

The breeze was, indeed, lifting the early morning mist, offering gradually a landscape of hills and valleys in muted colours of browns, greens, greys and purple. Now and again a rabbit broke cover, sometimes a grouse or partridge flew out of the undergrowth and took to the sky, but no shots were taken, nor had there been any for two days previously in order that the deer were not disturbed for this day's sport.

They breached the summit of Ardbeg, still not

talking, saving their breath for the climb, and
Stuart raked the further hills with the glasses and
beckoned them on. They skirted the next hill and
he cautioned them with a lifted finger and made
his way stealthily to the brow of a rocky ridge. He
lay for a few moments, scanning beyond and then
returned to them.

'We've found them, and Zeus is in the group.
Come and see for yourselves.'

They all carefully made their way to the ridge
and peered over. Alex, with glasses raised to his
eyes, murmured, 'I see them. Difficult to pick out
in the heather and rock, aren't they? Wonderful
camouflage. I gather Zeus is the grand beast
nearest to us?'

Stuart nodded and passed his glasses to Agnes.
'Lovely Old Zeus,' she breathed, admiring the
graceful line of the stag before handing the glasses
on to Jean. 'You have a long stalk ahead of you,
Alex. They must be over a mile away, don't you
think, Stu?'

Stuart grunted agreement. 'We'll make for
Ardbeg bothy for lunch as arranged. The wind
direction has changed slightly which means a
detour so they don't pick up our scent. Are you
still game, Alex?' he asked, and his voice,
although friendly enough, had an edge of challenge to it.

Alex responded whimsically, 'I'll try not to fall
by the wayside.'

Agnes regarded Stuart with a flicker of anxiety.

His remark was so unlike him that she wondered if he suspected how she felt about Alex.

Lunch had been left for them by Hector in the bothy—a small wooden hut used by shepherds as a refuge. The lunch basket was brought outside and they consumed sandwiches and tea, enjoying a break in the clouds through which a pale sun shone bravely.

'Any blisters needing attention?' Stuart asked as the girls repacked the basket and put it inside the bothy for the gillies to collect later. Everyone assured him they were blister-free, so he declared, 'Time to go, then.'

'Nature calls,' Agnes said firmly, and walked off into the scrub, making for a outcrop of rock some yards away.

Jean scrambled to her feet and followed. 'You make it so easy,' she told Agnes, laughing a little.

Agnes grinned. 'We can't be embarrassed with Stuart, can we? We've known him too long, and I'm damned if I'm going to be uncomfortable all day for fear of offending Alex's delicate sensibilities, which I doubt he has anyway.'

On their return, Jean gasped, 'Oh, lor' we'd better hurry, they're waiting for us,' and she began to run. Agnes sighed a smile, not altering her pace, realising that Jean would never change, always bending her will to other people, Stuart especially. Suddenly her friend fell to the ground with a sharp cry and Agnes broke into a run, reaching her first, demanding, 'Jean—are you all right?'

'My ankle,' groaned Jean, white-faced with pain. 'How could I be so stupid?' She added wretchedly, 'A stupid rabbit hole and I have to find it!'

By this time Stuart and Alex had arrived on the scene and Stuart said, 'Agnes, get the first aid box from the bothy, will you?' He knelt on the ground and carefully straightened Jean's leg. 'Let's have a look, Jean. I'll try not to hurt you.' Alex laid Stuart's rifle, with his own, on the ground out of harm's way and knelt down on the other side.

Jean bit her lip and grimaced as Stuart eased off her sock and shoe. 'I'm sure I'll be able to carry on in a minute,' she said.

Stuart retorted with cousinly frankness, 'Don't talk rubbish, Jean.'

Nearly in tears, she claimed, 'I've ruined the day.' When Agnes came back with the box she took one of Jean's hands and squeezed it reasuringly.

'Is there any water handy; we ought to try and get the swelling down,' suggested Alex. Stuart nodded and set off for a tiny stream they had recently crossed.

'Can you move your toes?' Alex asked, feeling the ankle and foot with gentle fingers, and Jean showed him that she could. 'I'm sure nothing is broken,' he went on, giving her a smile, 'and that it's merely a bad sprain.' Jean gave him a wan smile in return. Stuart arrived back and wrapped his wet scarf round her ankle. He took a flask from his anorak pocket and urged Jean to take a drink.

Spluttering from the potency of the brandy, but with colour coming slowly back to her face, Jean said remorsefully, 'Alex, I'm so very sorry, spoiling everything——'

'But you haven't,' he broke in firmly. 'I've enjoyed myself immensely so far, and there's always another day.'

'Of course there is,' agreed Stuart, frowning thoughtfully, 'and, in any event, all is not lost. Jean and I will wait for the gillie to arrive to fetch lunch. He'll have a pony with him which Jean can ride back to the Land Rover. Then I'll drive her on to Ard House and we'll decide then whether she needs to have it looked at professionally.'

'Couldn't I stay with her instead of you?' asked Agnes, knowing how much Stuart had been looking forward to the day's sport, and the prospect of being in Alex's company was hardly keeping a low profile in that respect. She handed crêpe bandages from the box to Alex who seemed to have taken over the task of dealing with Jean's ankle.

Stuart considered this, obviously tempted, and then declared, 'I'm not keen on you girls being left on your own—something might detain the gillie. No—I'll stay.' He eyed Jean's ankle, which was now bound, saying, 'I say, Alex you're making a good job of that, most professional.' He turned to address his tenant. 'Well, what do you say, Alex? Agnes knows these hills and I doubt she'll get you lost. It means you're still in with a chance for Old Zeus.'

Alex was studying Jean's face which was turned to his anxiously and gave a nod, giving his consent to the plan, and Jean immediately showed relief. The two men supported her back to the bothy where she was made comfortable on rugs, and, after Stuart had gone over with Agnes the principal landmarks she was to look out for, she and Alex set off, turning to wave goodbye at the point where their track led them out of sight.

They kept a fairly steady pace for over a mile before Agnes slowed down. 'Over that ridge, hopefully, will be your deer,' she told him, and then saved her breath for a steep climb. Taking the last stretch on hands and knees they finally were able to scan the terrain beyond.

'There they are, the beauties,' Alex murmured, glasses to eyes.

Agnes sneaked a glance at Alex watching the deer and realised just how much she was loving being on her own with him. She was sorry about Jean, of course, but she hadn't been alone with him since Stuart's return home. Now here she was, lying shoulder to shoulder, in an admittedly uncomfortable spot, miles from anyone, and she was happy. Idiotic, but what was the harm in a little self-indulgence occasionally?

Alex handed her the glasses, saying quietly,

'The wind is in our favour at the moment, so long as they don't take it into their heads to drift further over. We'll make for that tree stump.'

Agnes screwed up her nose and tucked a strand of escaped hair behind her ear. 'Mmm. . . I suspect the ground is boggy there, Alex, because of all that peat. Why don't we make for that rock slope? You should get as good a sighting from there.'

With narrowed eyes Alex considered this. 'Och, you're a grand wee bittie of a lassie, as Hector would say. He's trained you well. Your way it is.' He turned to look into her eyes.

Agnes felt her senses leap. Good grief! Here was a man who could actually accept a woman's advice! There was a lazy gleam in the grey depths as though he knew what she was thinking and she hastily reproved with mock severity, 'Flattery will not get you your stag. After you,' and she gestured him forward.

His smile was mocking as he touched his forelock in a pseudo-salute, drawling, 'As you say, ma'am.'

It was difficult going. Alex gained the top, Agnes coming after, conscious both of the care not to scrape their brogues on the surface or dislodge loose stones, which might have disturbed the deer and alerted them to their presence.

Alex put his mouth close to her ear and whispered, 'They're in range—our hour has come.' He paused. 'Did you know you have an incredibly fascinating ear, Aggie?' He teased it with the tip of his tongue.

'Folk stop me in the street just to tell me,' she whispered back, wondering how he could make such a ridiculous nickname sound so beautiful.

'Concentrate,' she admonished, her eyes fixed on the deer who were grazing in a desultory manner. The tickling stopped and she heard him give a soft sigh before turning his attention back to the animals.

It was certainly Old Zeus who drew the eye. He was a magnificent beast, noble, graceful, the red-brown of his hide and the formation of his fine set of antlers making a wonderful picture against the background of sky and hills.

Agnes held her breath. She had no doubt that Alex was a good shot and he was in perfect range and yet it was still anyone's game. Her eyes went carefully to Alex. She saw his finger take up the tension on the trigger. Old Zeus stood motionless, totally vulnerable. Suddenly it was too much for her and she clutched Alex's shoulder convulsively.

'No, Alex, no!'

The smack of a shot rang out and echoed round the hills. Old Zeus's head went up and he gave a huge leap forward. Agnes thought—he's got him! And then all four deer were fleeing for all they were worth, bounding in huge lifts through the heather. There was a long stillness as if everything was suspended. Alex swung towards her, his eyes ablaze with anger.

'What the hell did you do that for?' He broke open the rifle and dropped it beside him on a bed of heather. 'All the effort we put into that stalk just thrown away.'

'I don't know. Old Zeus is special somehow. I—couldn't help myself.'

'Well, you certainly didn't help me. Or Old Zeus either, come to that. His time's nearly up, however he goes.'

He sprang to his feet, picked up the rifle with one hand and grabbed her arm with the other dragging her with him. Then suddenly he stopped, released her and said in a milder tone, 'I shall have to make my peace with Hector. But, truth to tell, I didn't want him to die either. So you needn't reproach yourself.' He took her arm again, but gently this time and resumed the march.

'We'd better get on.'

Agnes repressed a smile and set off, constantly checking their route, for she didn't want them to get lost. Half an hour later they reached the summit and beyond was downhill all the way. The track was reasonable and they were walking abreast, discussing the parts of Scotland they had both visited, when suddenly, without warning, the pale sunlight was wiped out, along with the view of the valley, by a blank opaque mass. Agnes clutched Alex's arm and they stood still, unable to see more than two paces in front of them.

'How extraordinary,' exclaimed Alex, and he turned his head and smiled at her. There was something extremely reassuring about the calm expression on his face. The mist swirled, lifted a little, and then thickened once more. An eerie silence surrounded them.

Although it had happened more than once to her, Agnes could never quite get used to the almost supernatural atmosphere that prevailed during such incidents and she mentioned this to Alex.

'Witches and phantom horsemen?' he suggested. 'Hum. . .you have a vivid imagination, my girl. We can't stand here forever. . . I noticed an overhang of rocks about a stone's throw to the left of us. The next time the mist gives us a chance, we'll make for it, mm?'

Agnes nodded. She glanced up and noticed moisture glistening in droplets on his eyebrows and hair and guessed that her own would be the same.

'It's moving,' Alex said. 'Off we go.' They crossed the cushion of peat and moss, holding each other firmly, and, by the time they gained their sanctuary, the mist had dropped and curtained them off once more.

'Shall we sit and make ourselves comfortable?' he suggested, and then added, 'Comfortable, I said.' There was a smile in his voice as he tucked her into the curve of his arm. Agnes was not going to argue. The air was chill, she shivered, and he added quickly, 'Are you cold? Here, give me your hands.' He took them and enveloped them in his own. 'How long can this last?'

'Anything from a quarter of an hour to all night.' Agnes was thinking of Hector, waiting for them, and hoped he wouldn't worry.

Alex stared into the mist assessingly. 'There's a current of air so I guess it could lift as suddenly as it came down.' He dug into his pocket and brought out a peppermint, offering it to her.

'A man of resources,' marvelled Agnes, popping it into her mouth and then she froze, clutching his forearm in a warning grip. 'Alex! What's that?'

A clink, like the sound of steel on steel, a snort from an animal and four barely discernible masses loomed up out of the grey-whiteness and passed by, like ghosts.

Agnes didn't realise she was holding her breath until she let it out, laughing a little, as she murmured, 'How spooky!'

'You'd almost got me thinking in terms of the supernatural—Highland clan battles, the lot! And all it was——'

'Was Old Zeus and his consorts,' chuckled Agnes. 'The hairs on the back of my neck actually bristled.'

'"Double, double toil and trouble; Fire burn and

cauldron bubble,"' Alex intoned to awesome effect.

'"Lizard's leg, and howlet's wing, for a charm of powerful trouble, like a hell-broth boil and bubble,"' emoted Agnes eerily, and she gave a smirk. 'I was second witch in the school production of Macbeth.' She tilted her head at him. 'A fan of dear old Shakespeare, are you?'

'We men from the backwoods know a bit of culture when we see it,' he answered her reproachfully, and went on lyrically, '"How silver-sweet sound lovers' tongues by night, like softest music to attenting ears!"'

'Alex! You were never Romeo!' gurgled Agnes, dissolving into chuckles. 'An old cynic like you— I don't believe it.'

'A lapse in my youth. I must admit that my legs were skinny in tights, but I'd have you know that my Romeo has gone down in the annals of history. Mostly for getting the aforementioned garment hooked on to the balcony trellis. Yes, you may laugh, but it was a painful and tricky few seconds.' He waited until she had stopped giggling and added, 'I'm deeply hurt at your response, and suggest we change the subject.'

'I agree,' said Agnes promptly. 'We——'

Alex leaned forward gathering her close and stopped her words with a kiss. When the kiss was finished—and it was no rushed job—he observed, 'This is much better than talking, don't you think?' and he kissed her again, warming to his theme, and then leaned back a little, viewing her flushed face and uneven breathing with teasing satisfaction, drawling lazily, 'What a lucky day it's been for us, Aggie. . . Jean kindly spraining her ankle, the mist obliging at the right moment. I suggest we diagnose how your mouth curves quite bewitchingly, as it's doing now, simply asking to be kis——'

'It was a lucky day for Old Zeus too,' asserted Agnes breathlessly, spreading her palms against his chest, 'and I think I should point out that the mist is lifting.'

'Mmm? Nonsense, you're imagining it,' came his firm response. He adopted a pedantic tone. 'As a scientist, my dear, I really do need to carry on with my experiments. . . They are of international importance. My thesis on mouths I have loved. . .'

Laughing, she said, 'I'm sure you're an authority, Professor, but the mist is definitely lifting. We still have at least four miles to go and I don't want Hector sending out a search party for us.' She scrambled to her feet as his arms released her at once.

Alex groaned, the groan deepening as he staggered upright.

'We shall adjourn and continue in more comfortable and warmer climes; my bones are creaking with the damp. I can't be as fit as I thought I was, but I'm darned if I'm going to let a slip of a girl finish the course without me.'

'That's the spirit,' Agnes encouraged cheerfully, knowing he could walk her into the ground. She stretched her arms and legs, and, finding she could see as far as the track, made her way over to it, Alex following close behind. Suddenly the view opened up before them. It was quite startling, being trapped one minute and having a vast panorama dropping away only yards from their feet the next.

Agnes had barely taken a few steps further when she stopped and fell to her knees in the scrub, crying in delight, 'Why, Alex, white heather! See?'

He watched her break off a single stem, taking care not to disturb the root. 'Is it special?' he asked.

'Very special,' she replied, straightening, eyes shining. 'I've never found any before, in all the years I've walked these mountains.' She looked back at their rocky shelter. 'We didn't know it, but we were quite safe from the evil spirits. This would have protected us from any danger.'

'How nice to know,' he said gravely, his eyes taking in her animated face.

'This is supposed to have the power to grant a wish,' she told him as they began to walk along the track. She put the sprig carefully into her pocket. 'There's a story, a legend from way back, about a warrior hero who lay dying, and he gave one of his followers a sprig of purple heather, telling the man to take it to his sweetheart as a token of his love. When her tears fell on the flowers they turned white, and, ever since, white heather has been the symbol of faithful love.' She gave him a challenging look. 'Isn't that romantic?'

'Devastating,' was the laconic reply.

Agnes grinned, told him to put his best foot forward, and, ignoring the blister that was beginning to hurt like mad on her right foot, saved her breath for the hike home. Now and again she caught Alex's eye and they exchanged smiles. As they walked she thought about Zeus, glad that Alex had forgiven her for interfering. She thought she understood why. He had had a great deal of personal pleasure in tracking the animal down, and killing it would not have increased that pleasure. Her respect for him grew.

'I think we'll stop and put a plaster on that blister,' Alex said, and he applied one to her heel, scolding her amiably for not telling him sooner. From then on they walked with her arm through his.

'Nearly there,' Agnes announced as they rounded a bend and saw the Land Rover in the distance, weariness making her stumble.

'Thank you for showing me your mountains,' Alex said. He tugged her hair gently. 'You make a spunky guide. I'm sorry we're not coming home more triumphantly.'

'I feel quite triumphant, thank you,' Agnes declared and his brows rose.

'Do you? I wonder why?' He waved to the

figure standing by the side of the van and received a shouted greeting in return. As they approached, Hector said, 'Bad luck, Mr Brandon. We had you in the glasses and thought you had him for a minute. The breeze shifted slightly, maybe, and he caught your scent?' Hector's voice was gentle.

'No, Hector,' Alex replied easily. 'He was a sitting target and I bungled it.'

Hector's phlegmatic gaze went from Alex to Agnes and back again.

'Aye, it can happen,' he agreed, his face bland. 'The Laird didna wait.' Hector opened the Land Rover door. 'When we saw the mist coming down we knew you would stay put for a wee while.'

Agnes dragged herself on to the seat, Alex squeezing beside her.

Hector went on, 'The Laird says you're to take a bath at the Big House, Miss Agnes, knowing you haven't the facilities at Cluny.' He slid behind the wheel. 'You did well today, lassie.'

Alex murmured his agreement and Agnes smiled and yawned. 'How's Jean?' she asked.

Hector replied. 'The swelling has gone down and she's feeling much better.'

Agnes yawned again and murmured, 'Oh, good,' and during the drive back she nearly dropped off to sleep, her head resting on Alex's shoulder, but just stayed on the edge of consciousness. It had been a lovely day. They had done well to get so close to Old Zeus and she was glad he was still out there somewhere. She had received praise from Hector, which was like being given a prize, and Alex had called her spunky. . . Alex. She would have to think about him another time when she wasn't so tired, but it was nice being propped up against him in the confines of the front seat, his arm protecting her from being shaken about.

As the Land Rover drew up at Ard House, Stuart came out to meet them. Alex jumped down and stood aside as Stuart helped Agnes from the seat, supporting her as her legs gave way.

'Poor old thing,' he commiserated, 'are you stiffening up?' He glanced at Alex. 'Sorry you weren't lucky with old Zeus. Another time, maybe.'

Agnes heard Alex murmur something appropriate and she smiled at him, not able to see his face properly in the darkness, and called goodnight as she allowed Stuart to help her into the house.

Stuart grinned as he watched her give another huge yawn and he gave her a hug, saying proudly, 'Full marks, Agnes—couldn't have done better myself.'

'Why, Stu! Can I have that in writing?' she mocked, smiling.

'What was he like?' Stuart asked casually.

'Who—Alex? Oh, a good stalker.' Agnes stepped up on to the first stair. 'Knows what he's doing.'

'I bet he was mad when he missed.' There was

a hint of satisfaction in his voice which, on reflection, Agnes thought was justified. 'You and Hector thought he'd bring it off, didn't you?' Stuart added with a knowing smile.

'Mm. . .yes, we did.'

'And you were both wrong,' he stated cheerfully.

Agnes smiled and made no reply to that. She blew out a long breath. 'I'm for that bath,' she announced and slowly began to climb the stairs.

Stuart watched her go, his face thoughtful.

CHAPTER SIX

A NOTE from the Dower House was dropped through the letter-box asking Agnes to dine in two days' time. From Kirsten Agnes learned that Alex had left Ardneath to collect his brother, who was coming to stay for a while.

Agnes was curious; families were important. Meeting Alex's brother might mean that a little more of him could be slotted into place.

With Jean being restricted by her sprained ankle Agnes spent more time helping out at Ard House and so she didn't meet the new Brandon before the dinner party, although word came by Kirsten that he had arrived.

Agnes decided to walk to the Dower House, admiring the setting sun which gave an incredibly rosy glow over the woods and hills and the waters of the loch. She was wearing a deceptively simple strappy dress, terracotta in colour, which added to the bloom of her skin and showed to advantage her narrow waist. The skirt was cut on the bias and swirled when she walked. For later in the evening, when it would turn cooler, she carried an Indian shawl in creams and browns and a matching shade to her dress. All of which, she had decided, viewing herself in the mirror, should dispel the scruffy image created by the T-shirt, baggy sweater and various other shapeless casual clothes she had been sporting that holiday.

The Dower House front door was open and a delicious smell of cooking wafted from the kitchen, indicating that Kirsten was in residence. As Agnes stepped into the hall a figure loomed up in the half light, coming from an inner room, and her pulse quickened. As he came further into the light she saw that it wasn't Alex—this was a slightly younger man, with dark curly hair and blue eyes.

These eyes were looking at her with frank curiosity. 'Ah! Good. It's Agnes Quinn, am I right?' he exclaimed, taking her hand in a friendly hand clasp. 'Zander was just about to start out to look for you—let me take your wrap, shall I?' He grinned. 'I haven't introduced myself, have I. I'm Zander's brother, Barnaby. Come and let me get you a drink.' He led her into the room he had just vacated, leading her over to a drinks table in the corner.

It was a room she knew well, having the faded gentility that was echoed in Ard House. Good quality furnishings that had seen a better day, but which still had charm and style. Agnes had long wanted, professionally, to get her hands on the whole house and return it to how it once had been.

One swift glance told her that Alex was not in the room. Stuart and Jean were; Jean with her foot resting on a stool, Stuart standing by her chair talking to a third person, a woman who looked to be in her middle thirties.

'I'll introduce you in a minute,' Barnaby promised, pouring out the sherry she had asked for, 'but you'll need this first,' and he gave her the glass. 'We Brandons are a bit much to take without a little help.'

Agnes smiled, responding to his relaxed, friendly manner. 'I don't believe that,' she said.

'I guess I'm comparatively easy to take, although Zander says I talk too much.' And his eyes crinkled teasingly. He gave the room a sweeping glance. 'I must say I'm pleasantly surprised,' he confessed without a qualm. 'I was expecting to meet a lot of old fuddy-duddies here tonight. Old crofters with white hair and little elderly ladies spinning by the fire.'

'There are a few around,' Agnes conceded with a smile, 'if you know where to look.'

'You're not shocked, are you?' stated Barnaby comfortably. 'I can always tell.'

'I don't shock easily,' agreed Agnes, adding, 'How long are you staying at Ardneath?'

'The least possible time,' replied Barnaby drolly. 'I'm only here on sufferance. Zander thinks it's a good idea for us to get to know the country of our ancestors and I guess I agree really, but, to be honest, I prefer the city to the country any day.' His face lit up. 'But to please Zander, who is a great older brother, I'm being good and filling space here in Ardneath for a while.'

Agnes was charmed. Barnaby bubbled and sparkled and was so disarming. She warmed immediately to him and to hear him call Alex by the endearing name of Zander delighted her.

'It's all very beautiful, of course,' Barnaby went on, 'but I'm just not into scenery—any scenery. I'm a city person and that's all there is to it. But at least there's a real live chieftain here in person, and wearing the kilt too—a wow with the girls, don't you think?' And his laughing eyes turned to Agnes a slanting glance full of speculation.

'Really, Barny, you strain a person's politeness to the limit.'

Agnes gave a little jump, which she hoped wasn't noticed, as a voice, dry and compelling, interrupted from behind and Alex moved into view.

'Good evening, Agnes—glad you could come.'

'Hello, Alex, thank you for asking me.' Her manner was as polite as his, but, try as she might to remain composed, Agnes found that her heart was beating faster. She had forgotten what it was like to have her body switched on as easily and as simply as switching on a light bulb. For this to happen at all was unusual, but for it to happen in so short a time and just for the sound of his voice and a glance from his grey eyes was mind-blowing.

Barnaby's smile broadened as he looked from one to the other.

'Don't worry, Zander, she's quite capable of telling me to mind my own business, aren't you, Agnes?' And without waiting for a reply he left them and joined Stuart and Jean.

'Barnaby tends to leave a trail of havoc behind him for the hell of it,' Alex offered drily, 'but there's no malice in his nature.'

'I'm sure there isn't,' Agnes said.

She had become used to seeing him in comfortable, well-worn casual gear suitable for rambling about in the country, but tonight Alex was wearing a pale grey suit teamed with a striped shirt and no tie, all modern and designer-made. Soft white leather shoes and a red handkerchief hanging from the jacket top pocket completed the ensemble. All this she had taken in on her first swift glance and she was reminded of the taciturn stranger on the Highland road and the large heavy spots of rain darkening an impeccable grey suit and the needle of the petrol gauge refusing to move.

She found they were smiling at each other in a silence that was crowded with unspoken words.

'Do introduce me, Alex, darling,' a cool voice commanded, and the brunette who previously had been talking to Stuart now settled herself at Alex's side, gazing with shrewd, curious eyes at Agnes.

'Sorry, Nadine,' Alex replied, swinging his eyes

from Agnes to her leisurely. 'I thought Barnaby had looked after all that.' He went through the motions, mentioning that Agnes had the pretty cottage near the bridge which he had pointed out to Nadine the day before, and was the possessor of the bees from which came her breakfast honey, and then describing Nadine as an old family friend.

This Nadine seemed compelled to enlarge upon. 'We Cartiers have been connected with the Brandons, one way or another, for years, haven't we, Alex?' she said, smiling up at him and tucking her arm through his. She turned her elegant head to offer Agnes the remains of the smile.

'Nadine works in Vancouver for the family publishing firm,' Alex explained, refilling their glasses.

Tapping an exquisitely manicured finger on his arm, Nadine said, 'I'm combining vacation with business on this trip. I'm longing to explore Edinburgh when my business in London is done. Alex has promised to show me around.' The smile again flashed upwards to Alex's face. She turned back to Agnes, asking, 'Are you on vacation, Agnes?'

Agnes nodded. 'It's nearly over, though—I go back home on Sunday.'

'And then work?' Nadine enquired, and when Agnes admitted that this was the case, and, to another question, that she was a fabric designer, Nadine observed, 'How interesting.'

Agnes thought, You don't care a damn what I do, or who I am, only how I'm concerned with the Brandons, and Alex in particular, and about that you're not sure. It was then that Agnes gave a mocking inward laugh at herself, thinking, Lady—at this moment that makes two of us!

Her eyes caught Alex's. He was regarding her beneath drooped lids, an amused gleam in their depths, and once more she had the ridiculous feeling that he could read her mind.

'I say, Zander, Kirsten says we can eat.' Barnaby came up and offered Agnes his arm, drawing her away with an 'Excuse us,' and smiling as if he was enjoying a secret joke. 'I hope you're hungry,' he said.

'I am—my stomach's beginning to rumble,' confessed Agnes, walking with him into the dining-room where Kirsten had done the large oval table proud, bringing out the best glasses and table linens and polishing the silver until it sparkled in the candlelight. She felt a sentimental glow in being part of Ardneath and Cameron roots and she turned and exchanged a smile with Stuart who was following behind her.

Barnaby pulled out a chair for her, saying, 'Good. I like a healthy appetite and you're next to me.'

Opposite, with Nadine at his side, Alex's sardonic features were thoughtful as he regarded Barnaby and herself and she sensed something, some form of unspoken communication, pass between the two brothers before their duties as hosts broke contact.

Agnes was able to study Nadine at leisure. She was attractive in a slightly hard, perfect way, Agnes admitted. She was beautifully made-up and wore her hair in a smooth chignon, and her black dress had probably been designed for her. And were those real diamonds at her throat and wrist? Maybe she was a touch too perfect—or maybe I'm a touch too envious, Agnes decided with wry honesty, envious not of how she looked but of the intimate way Nadine was now smiling at Alex.

This won't do, Agnes scolded herself, and turned to Barnaby to ask, 'Is this your first time in Scotland?'

He shook his head. 'I came over with friends when I was twenty and we footed it any way we could, all over Europe, for three months, Scotland included. It was a terrific experience.' He filled her glass with white wine and waited as Kirsten, frowning in concentration, served the fish course. 'Zander was telling me you were practically brought up here at Ardneath, but that you're English.'

Agnes felt a streak of pleasure rush through her at the thought that Alex had been speaking of her to his brother. 'My career means that I have to live in Edinburgh and I can only get here for short spells, but the glen holds part of me, and I suspect always will.'

With skilful questioning Barnaby extracted an

incredible amount of information from her, about herself, her business, her hopes and aspirations, until she suddenly realised just how much she had been talking, and exclaimed laughingly, 'Hey, that's enough about me. Tell me something of yourself.'

'What do you want to know?' Barnaby leaned back in his chair and spread his hands expansively. 'I'm twenty-eight, unmarried, enjoy most sports and travel and am in Edinburgh setting up a branch of the family business.' He saw the surprise on her face and added, 'Alex, I gather, hasn't said anything about it.'

Agnes said drily, 'Your brother isn't very forthcoming about himself.'

Barnaby grinned a little absently and his eyes travelled across the table to the brother in question, who was encouraging Jean to talk to him. 'He has a good line in reticence, hasn't he?' he agreed. 'I don't know where he gets it from because I do my fair share of gabbing. . .and maybe that's why.' He took a sip of his wine, leaning back to allow Kirsten to place the main course in front of them. When she had moved on, Barnaby went on, 'As for the family business, we're merchant bankers.'

Agnes stared at him, digesting this piece of information. 'Merchant bankers,' she said slowly. 'Does that mean you deal with companies rather than individuals?' She shook her head a little and gave a small laugh. 'I never dreamed Alex was a banker.'

'He's not,' said Barnaby. 'He's a doctor.'

Agnes was taking wine as he made this extraordinary statement and it went down the wrong way. As she spluttered for breath Barnaby patted her back anxiously and everyone stopped talking. With brimming eyes Agnes assured them she was all right and Alex said drily, 'What are you doing to the poor girl, Barny?'

Before Barnaby could protest, Agnes broke in with, 'He's looking after me beautifully, and I'm finding him extremely interesting.' She allowed her eyes to hold Alex's for a second, meaningfully, and his expression became fleetingly ironic. The moment passed and everyone carried on as before.

'Does it surprise you that much?' Barnaby asked. 'He's a darned good doctor.'

'I'm sure he is,' said Agnes, remembering the gentle, confident way he had bound up Jean's ankle. 'And now I know, it seems perfectly feasible. He said he was between jobs at the moment and went on to list a few he'd done in the past but they were obviously jobs taken when he was a young man. . .'

'Yeah, that's right.' Barnaby grinned. 'We had to take vac jobs when we were at college.'

'Somehow I never bothered to ask him outright.'

'He is between jobs. . .he's due to start a post

in Edinburgh at the hospital and university, teaching and researching. Quite the brainy bod is our Zander. Genetics, that's what he's specialising in.'

Agnes nodded and while the choice of pudding was discussed round the table she thought about what Barnaby had told her. Alex, a doctor. Lecturer and research scientist in the field of genetics. She puzzled over what she knew about genes. Nothing more than what she had learned in biology lessons at school. She searched her memory and remembered a little—that genes were the carriers of hereditary factors in the cells of the body. So many chromosomes in each cell. She felt a sense of achievement and smiled to herself. She glanced across at him, her expression thoughtful, and he caught her look. His eyes moved to Barnaby and back again and his brows rose.

You're not the only one to be enigmatic, Agnes thought, giving him back stare for stare in what she hoped was a good example.

Barnaby whispered, 'Oh, boy, I think I'm going to be in trouble for opening my big mouth.'

'Just take comfort that he could be in the firing line too,' soothed Agnes, and Barnaby shot her an uncertain look.

Nadine was at Alex's side for coffee later in the sitting room and Barnaby whispered in Agnes' ear, 'Awful, isn't she? So bloody patronising. If she marries Zander I'll throw up!'

'Is she likely to?'

Agnes glanced to where Nadine was laughing

at something Alex was saying and felt a funny lurch of her heart.

'They were pretty thick when Zander was at medical school—that was years ago, of course. She has been married but got rid of the poor chap for some reason, but I think she's set her sights on him. I like to think he's got more sense, but some of the most extraordinary people get together.'

'Are you sure you should be telling me this, Barny?' asked Agnes.

Barnaby grinned. 'I should have thought it was pretty obvious. She's stuck to him like a limpet since we arrived. I'm awfully fond of Zander. I'd hate to see him make the wrong choice.'

So would Agnes, but there was nothing she could do to influence matters. After all, Alex was a free agent. She did her best to ignore Nadine at his side hanging on to his every word. Determinedly bright, she laughed and talked, drawing Stuart and Jean into a discussion about their Scottish heritage for Barnaby's benefit.

'We're descended from the clan of Fraser,' Barnaby offered, not without a little pride, 'And we've been known to wear Fraser colours now and again, even though we've been settled in Canada for over four generations.'

'Fellow Jacobites,' said Jean, pleased. 'How nice that we're not sworn enemies.' And everyone laughed.

As talk went on around her, Agnes fell silent. She had much to occupy her thoughts and as they were mostly concerning Alex it was natural that her gaze should seek him out.

He was standing at the far side of the room, now talking to Stuart. Some adjustment needed to take place with Barnaby's surprising news. Yes, it was easy to see Alex as a doctor. He had a cool, calm detachment, a considering way of thinking things through, and she thought his quiet authority would instil confidence. And then as a teacher those same attributes would hold good.

It was difficult to recall much of the rest of the evening at Dower House except that Agnes was sensitive to everything Alex said or did. Even if she was not in direct contact with him there was not a moment when she was not aware of what he was doing, not an expression or an opinion with which she could not identify.

At one point she remembered that Jean whispered, 'Are you all right, Agnes? You've gone quiet.'

Agnes had replied hastily. 'I'm fine, Jean,' while thinking wryly that she should have said—I'm smitten with that dangerous disease called love. It's in its early stages, but it could prove fatal. She imagined Jean's face if she had given in to the impulse.

'Barnaby's fun, isn't he?' Jean went on. 'He's persuaded Stuart into organising a picnic on the island tomorrow if it's fine.' Her eyes travelled to Nadine. 'I'm not so sure that I like Miss Cartier, but everyone else has been sweet to me all evening. I don't think I've talked so much to anyone for ages.'

When it was time for the guests to make a move, Stuart asked Agnes, 'Did you walk over, Agnes? Like a lift back?'

Before she could answer, Alex broke in smoothly, 'Thanks, Stuart, but we'll take care of her.'

And Stuart nodded. He could hardly argue with his host. He waited a moment to see if Agnes had anything to say to that, and, when she remained silent, he called a general goodnight and left with Jean.

'Shall I run Agnes home, Zander?' suggested Barnaby, picking up her shawl.

'Go to bed, baby brother. Agnes is my responsibility,' Alex said firmly, taking the shawl from him and dropping it lightly across her shoulders. Agnes was conscious of Nadine's disapproval of the gesture.

The XJS was standing in the drive. They did not talk as Alex settled her into her seat and it was not until he was driving slowly along the loch road that he asked,

'What do you think of my baby brother?' He shot her a swift, quizzical glance.

'Barnaby? I thought him charming, intelligent, amusing. . .'

'The devil you did,' Alex murmured with a distinctive drawl.

'And most informative.' Agnes turned her head to look at him, her voice dulcet.

'I thought he was. I might tell you that you were supposed to be sitting next to me—that was what we arranged beforehand—but someone did a spot of rearranging. And I'm wondering why.'

Someone. Nadine? Or Barnaby?

'It couldn't be that Barnaby fell in love with my eyes?'

'He'd have a job not to, but we Brandons are the faithful type and Barny has a girl back home.'

The headlights showed up Cluny Cottage in their beam and Alex slowed the car to a halt. The engine died and there was quiet for a moment and then he asked, 'Mad at me?'

'I haven't decided yet,' Agnes said. She saw by the pale moonlight filtering through into the car that he was watching her thoughtfully.

'What did baby brother tell you?' he asked at last.

'Oh, quite unimportant snippets,' she answered airily. 'Things like you're a doctor; that your family business is merchant banking.'

'Barny definitely talks too much,' Alex stated drily. He took her hand, the one nearest to him, and studied it as if he had never seen a hand before.

'I was going to tell you all that soon, in my own time and place. Ardneath has been a bolt-hole, a place where I've shed my past and shelved my future. I've been marking time, Agnes. No responsibilities—a simple existence. It was unrealistic of me to think that once Barnaby invaded the glen things could stay the same, and it's strange, but I'd forgotten how little you knew of me. It hardly seemed important. I don't expect you to understand.'

'But I do,' she said. Her hand was sizzling wildly in his, a current of awareness running between them.

He raised her hand and put it gently to his lips.

'I rarely tell anyone I'm a doctor at first meeting. You'd be surprised at how many impromptu consultations I'd have if I did. Perfect strangers open up the minute they know and all their ailments are thrown at me.' He laughed softly. 'Of course, it's possible, on rare occasions, to find a stranger more perfect than the rest, who makes you forget that you are a doctor or even the time of day.'

His thumb lightly stroked her hand. 'Barny, I guess, told you I'll be working in Edinburgh. You're there too.' His voice embraced her with promises. 'I hope you've had the Morgan's float fixed for your journey home?'

'I have,' confirmed Agnes smiling, savouring the words, the glance, the unspoken promises. 'Don't remind me what an idiot I was, please!'

'No, I won't, because I can only remember a spunky, challenging girl who was so mad at herself she could have wept!' His lips curved, the creases deepening in his cheeks. 'Hopping mad at having to ask for my help. . .'

'Oh, I was! And you annoyed and intrigued me in equal parts,' Agnes confessed, laughing softly.

'Then, when you finally told me your name, I knew I'd be seeing you again.' He twisted slightly in his seat so that he could face her. 'You see, I knew from Kirsten and Hector that you were coming. I was only mildly interested. The name Agnes Quinn meant nothing to me. But that was because I hadn't met you and didn't know you were funny and adorable and irresistible, with huge amber eyes and a mass of wild sunshine hair; that you were warm and compassionate, courageous and intelligent, stubborn and very, very desirable. . .' He touched her hair, lifting it from her face and letting it drift back into place. 'But they didn't tell me and so how could I guess?'

The words flowed over her and Agnes listened with increasing wonder and delight, the blood whooshing to her head as if she had drunk a bottle of champagne. So he didn't care about Nadine after all. Laughter bubbled low in her throat as she teased, 'How remiss of them.'

And when his hand cupped the back of her neck she lifted her face to his and gave him her lips.

'I've been waiting to do that all night, among other things,' Alex murmured.

'Mm. . .so have I. What other things?' Agnes added, a smile in her voice.

'This is not the time to go into details, with my brother waiting back at the Dower House, no doubt timing my movements. I value my privacy too much.' He kissed her again and drew away reluctantly. 'I may not have another chance before you leave, so I'll take your telephone number now, shall I?' Alex brought out a diary from his jacket pocket.

Agnes collected her bemused thoughts and recited the number, thinking ahead to when they could be together in Edinburgh. Alex then scribbled on another page which he tore out and gave to her, saying, 'This is my address and number, I'm not sure when I'll be in the city—I have to spend some time with Barnaby—but I'll ring you the minute I get the chance.' He left the car and walked round to open the door for Agnes. She swung her legs out and he took her hands in his and lifted her up into his arms. They walked slowly up the path together, stopping at the front door where they merged into a close embrace. When Alex finally released her he said roughly, 'You'd better go in, or else my good intentions will take a tumble—and to hell with my brother and privacy!'

Agnes laughed happily and felt for the key above the lintel. Alex took it from her and unlocked the door, saying, as he did so, 'That would be the first place an intruder would look.'

'We don't get many intruders in Ardneath— just the occasional early morning snooper.'

'I was not snooping, dammit,' Alex said calmly, 'I was fishing—and I caught a water sprite.' He smoothed back the hair from her face and added, 'And very beautiful she was, too.' He kissed her eyes and then her mouth before handing her the key. 'You do lock the door behind you at night, I trust?' he asked, frowning a little.

'Yes,' she soothed, warmed by the concern in his voice. 'I also have Lass to guard me.' At the sound of her name, the lurcher bitch crept over from where she had been lying beneath a nearby bush, tail wagging. Agnes reached down and gave her some fuss. 'She comes every evening without fail and sleeps in the kennel at the back. When she hears me get up in the morning she shoots off back to the croft.'

'I admit she sets my mind at rest,' Alex said, and when Agnes straightened he searched her face, touching lightly the gentle hollow from cheekbone to chin.

The gesture, the touch, made her catch her breath, and she said wonderingly, 'This is ridiculous, isn't it? I mean, we hardly know each other.'

Alex acknowledged the truth of her statement with a droll lift of one brow and mused, 'But I think we both knew it could happen if we let it, didn't we?' Agnes motioned with her head her agreement, drinking in every loving detail, feature by feature, of his face. Not that it was necessary, for her artist's eye had memorised and stored each curve, line, shape and shade to be painted in her mind's eye whenever she was missing the real thing. 'As for getting to know each other,' Alex went on, 'that will soon be rectified. We shall let Edinburgh weave her spell over us, mm?' He kissed her, Agnes responding eagerly and with matching urgency, and there was a roughness in his voice as he said, 'Goodnight, Aggie. . .sweet Aggie,' and then he was away and striding down the path.

'Goodnight, Alexander,' called Agnes softly, watching him go. The XJS's lights were switched on and off rapidly in salute and the car made a precise three-point turn before purring quietly down the loch road in the direction of the Dower House.

'Alexander,' murmured Agnes, enjoying saying his name, and the watchful bitch moved the tip of her tail uncertainly, brown eyes fixed on Agnes's face. 'Alex. . .zander.' Agnes rolled it musically around her tongue with relish. 'Isn't he a lovely, lovely man, Lass?' And, pushing open the door, she went on, 'And he thinks I'm beautiful!' She looked back and could just see the red tail-light disappearing in the distance and with a silly smile on her lips she added dreamily, 'The poor fellow is wonderfully mad. . .'

CHAPTER SEVEN

THE day for the picnic dawned fair. Jean decided against going, as Agnes guessed she would, knowing her friend's dislike of both the island and the loch since Ian's death. Nadine joined them, wearing casual pants and jacket, managing to look as though she had stepped out of a fashion magazine.

Agnes was in practical gear: jeans, shirt and sweater. She found Barnaby fun and Stuart blossomed in his company, becoming part of the teasing camaraderie that was going on.

Even when Alex was not in her immediate company Agnes was happy. She secretly hugged to herself the memory of being in his arms only a few hours previously and disciplined herself to limit the number of times she looked at him. After the picnic lunch she found a corner in the ruined walls of the monastery and sat on a pile of stones, eyes closed, leaning back against what was once the bell tower. She heard the rattle of a stone and opened her eyes to see Stuart looking down at her.

She smiled up at him.

'It's lovely here, isn't it? I'll miss it all when I go back to Edinburgh.' She thought for a moment and then added idly, 'I say, Stuart, have I told you they're trying to throw me out of my tenancy?'

'Is that a fact?' He shot her a quick look of concern and then took both her hands in his, saying urgently, 'Then come back to Ardneath for good, Agnes. Make your home here and marry me.'

Heart sinking, Agnes said, 'Stuart, we've had all this out before ages ago and you know how I feel.'

'Don't give me any of that brother angle,' he came back impatiently. 'I'm not your brother and I don't want to be. I want to be your husband, Agnes.'

'And if I thought it was right, for both of us, I'd say yes, Stu, but it's not right.'

'I've always loved you, Agnes, even when we were kids, but it was always Ian with you, wasn't it?'

There was a stunned silence, both of them shocked by this sudden violent expression of his feelings. He took an obvious grip on his emotions and went on more quietly, but still with underlying passion. 'I hoped that, in time, I could fill his shoes. After all, we were twins. There can't be that much difference between us, for God's sake!'

Shock, pity, compassion even anger swept through Agnes in varying degrees, all liable to upset her balance of judgement, but, although she was distressed by the bitterness in his voice, she allowed none of her feelings to show in her reply.

'Don't say that, Stu. You must know how negative it is, thinking that way. You shouldn't be trying to fill Ian's shoes——'

'I've been doing that all my life, even when he was alive. I don't blame you for loving him. I loved him too.'

'You're a person in your own right, Stu, and I do love you—I admire and respect you, but I don't love you in the way you want me to. I wish you'd believe me. Oh, how stupid of me to keep coming back. It would be better if I stayed away, but I thought you'd got over all this——'

'Don't even think that! You'd really hurt me if you did that,' Stuart said angrily. 'Each time you came I wondered if I would see someone else's ring on your finger, and each time I gave a sigh of relief. I always hoped that one day. . .'

'That's no good, Stu. If you think there's a chance I'll eventually change my mind, then it stops you looking for someone else.' Agnes couldn't meet his eyes and turned her head away, staring into the distance, wondering where Alex had gone. He didn't seem to be with the others.

'And you've found that someone else,' Stuart said bitterly. 'I saw you last night, the way you were looking at him. It's Brandon, isn't it?'

There was silence between them and then Stuart sighed and turned away with a defeated air. 'They'll be wondering where we've got to.'

'You go on. I'll be with you shortly.'

Agnes sat quietly for a while after he had left

her as she thought about Ian, who had been her first love. Wonderful, charismatic, lovable Ian, whom she had idolised since she first set eyes on him and whose death had sent her nearly out of her mind with grief until she had learned, in time, to live with it. Had he lived, would she have married him and borne his children? She had only been seventeen. Would her love have grown and matured? Had she felt for Ian what she now felt for Alex Brandon? One thing was certain: she had always known that it would have been a mistake trying to recapture Ian through Stuart. Stuart was the brother she had never had. Nevertheless, his outburst had shaken her. She had thought he had accepted that they had no future together. Instead he had laid bare those soul-searching, painful feelings about her that must have been lying dormant for so long. Perhaps last night's party had shown him all too clearly that his hopes were empty ones. Agnes was filled with compassion for him, but compassion and love based on friendship were no basis on which to build a marriage.

There was no opportunity for further privacy with Alex, but he managed a quiet, 'I'll be in touch,' as he helped her down from the Land Rover when the day was over.

Agnes murmured, 'I'll be waiting,' before calling out her goodbyes to the others.

The following morning she found a sprig of white heather lying on the doorstep. There was no message, but none was needed.

Edinburgh was a beautiful city, built upon a series of hills, with more hills rising behind it and the sea lying at its feet. Agnes thought it was as if some theatrical director had built his giant stage and had manipulated nature to be his scenic designer. It was possible to catch sight of the hills or the sea from unexpected corners of the city and, as usual, when she arrived back, she glanced up at the castle, silhouetted against a darkening sky, remembering that a thousand years had passed since its creation.

The Old Town was crowded with history and a romantic hotch-potch of buildings going back to medieval times, while the New Town had its beginnings at the end of the eighteenth century and was graced with stately neo-Georgian architecture.

The street where Agnes lived was one of a row of Victorian houses all showing a dignified frontage to the outside world. These houses in their day used to be family residences, but the passing years had seen them change into apartments, and latterly into offices. They had retained their period façade, due to stringent planning rules, but only a handful now were still residential.

Agnes's was one of the few, although not for much longer. She struggled up the flight of stairs, carrying her things. The building was very quiet. As Agnes inserted her key she was aware of the fact that she was the only tenant left and that it was a good thing she was not the nervous sort.

As she walked into her sitting-room she felt a pang of regret for what they were trying to force her to leave. The room was spacious and she had decorated it herself, using her own fabric designs for the curtains and chair coverings, as she had the rest of the apartment, and it was annoying to think that she was going to have to start all over again somewhere else.

She half-heartedly picked up the pile of correspondence awaiting her attention which the cleaning lady had put in a neat stack on her desk. She skimmed through them, eyed the answering machine dourly, ignored it and went to run a bath. She lay in scented water and thought about Alex.

The following week flew by. Agnes was plunged into work with barely time to catch her breath. Cloth manufacturers needed to be contacted, warehouses visited, customers placated and cajoled, as well as time spent at the drawing-board. As the week neared its end each time the telephone rang she wondered if it would be Alex. She would pick it up and say, 'Anastasia Designs,' and in two seconds she would know a feeling of disappointment.

Even though the caller was not Alex, it wasn't always a disappointment. . .

'Anastasia Designs,' she announced one afternoon. It was a woman she had met and worked with before with work to put Agnes's way.

'A lovely job for you—one you'll enjoy

immensely. A total design job on a Queen Anne house in Regent Square. Owners returning soon from a posting in the Middle East. They're giving you *carte blanche*.'

An appointment was made to view the house. Good news but not the phone call Agnes wanted. That came finally when she had almost given up hope.

'Anastasia Designs.'

'Agnes? It's Alex.'

At the sound of those drawling vowels Agnes's heart leaped in her breast and proceeded to pump away at high speed. Their conversation was hardly brilliant, but it seemed to satisfy both participants.

'Hello, Alex.'

'I'm in Edinburgh.'

'Oh. good.'

'May we meet?'

'Yes, please.'

'Tonight? Could we eat?'

'Mm, yes, that'd be lovely.'

'The Pimpernel then; do you know it? Shall I pick you up?'

'Alex, do you mind if I meet you there?' Agnes said. 'I've promised to visit a friend in hospital but I could come on afterwards. Would eight suit?'

'It would suit very well. Until eight.' He paused and she could hear the smile in his voice as he said, 'Goodbye, Aggie.'

'I ought to be furious at you for calling me that,' she said severely.

'But you're not.'

'No. I can't think why.'

'I'll tell you some time.'

Agnes laughed softly. 'Goodbye, Alexander.' She put down the phone and let out a loud, 'Whoopee!' throwing her arms high as she whirled round and round until she collapsed into a chair. Suddenly the day was incredibly wonderful, and how she was going to get through the hours until eight she didn't know.

Holding a bunch of freesias in one hand and black grapes in the other, Agnes walked down the hospital ward, searching for the face of Vida Hope, friend and lawyer, among the sea of strange faces waiting expectantly for their visitors. Agnes spotted Vida and made for the bed. Her friend was lying on her stomach, eyes closed, and as she came close the lids shot up and a pair of eyes appraised her.

'Greetings, Vida,' Agnes said cheerfully. 'How are you? I thought you were supposed to be going home today? I was all set to visit you there until I got your message.'

'So I was,' answered Vida gloomily, 'but they changed their minds.'

'Bad luck,' soothed Agnes, pulling up a chair and sitting by the side of the bed. 'Are you in pain?'

'I'm in agony—at least, I was until the surgeon

wielded his knife and now life is a little easier.'
Vida scowled. 'I don't mind lying like this when I
have a choice, but when it's essential for comfort
then it becomes a bit much.' She eased herself up
on to her elbows. 'How can you get any sympathy
when you say you have a boil on your bum?
There! You see? Even you nearly smiled and
you're supposed to be my best mate.'

'It was a bit more than a boil, wasn't it?' Agnes
asked, laughing despite her good intentions.

'Yes, but it gets far too complicated to go into
gory details.' Vida flopped back on to her front. 'I
wonder why all visitors look so darned healthy—
it oughtn't to be allowed.' She gave Agnes a
searching look. 'You look wonderful, positively
blooming. Your holiday has obviously suited you.
At a guess I'd say that the glow and the stunning
dress—not put on for my benefit, of that I'm
sure—is all due to some man. Am I right?'

Agnes was strangely reluctant to answer. She
put the flowers and grapes on the locker top and
opened up the off-white coat so that Vida could
have a better view of the cranberry-coloured silk
dress she was wearing.

'You like it?' she asked.

'I like it,' Vida stated.

Agnes took pity on her. 'I had a wonderful
holiday, and yes, there's a man.'

'I knew it.' Satisfaction coloured Vida's voice
and then she added warily, 'It's not Stuart?'

Agnes gave an exasperated, 'Oh, Vida, of course not.'

'Just checking if he'd finally worn you down and you'd said yes because the glen expects it,' her friend confessed, unrepentant. 'So who is he? When did you meet? How old is he? What does he do? Is he gorgeous? Are you madly infatuated? Have you slept with him yet?'

Laughing, Agnes held up her hands to stem the flow. 'His name is Alexander——'

'I like it. Sounds a good, strong name.'

'We met at Ardneath. Yes, I think he's gorgeous: yes, I'm madly infatuated, and, no, I haven't slept with him, but everything comes to she who waits.'

'When do I meet him?'

Agnes grinned. 'Well, I could bring him here to see you, but I think you'd rather meet him a more dignified position.'

'You're right, I would. Agnes, tell me everything.'

'I shall tell you what I think is fit for your ears, Vida,' reproved Agnes, doing just that.

'White heather on your doorstep,' wondered Vida at the finish. 'My God! This proves that romance isn't dead.'

Agnes found pleasure in sharing Alex with Vida, something she would find it difficult to do with Jean. Jean was very loyal to Stuart and must know his hopes regarding Agnes although recently the two friends had not spoken of it.

'He sounds a hunk,' Vida declared. 'The minute I can sit decently in a chair I shall demand an interview. Canadian, eh? And a medical scientist. Rather interesting.' She slanted her friend a calculating look. 'Anything else I should know, Agnes?'

Agnes thought for a moment and then said innocently, 'He calls me Aggie.'

There was a stunned silence as Vida gaped, and she exclaimed in a hushed voice, 'Aggie? He actually calls you *Aggie*? And you haven't murdered him on the spot? Oh, Agnes!' The two friends exchanged grins and then, with a change of tone, Vida shot a look at the clock and said, 'Time's nearly up, so we'd better get down to business. I know you don't want to move. But, as your lawyer, I think you should take the Van Dreuse offer and vacate your apartment as soon as you can. They're offering a generous easement which can go towards the down payment on your new one.'

Agnes pulled a face. 'I'm sure you're right, Vida. I just don't want to go. How dare they assume that money will buy everything?' She blew out a cross breath. 'OK, I'll start looking round for another place.'

Vida gave a satisfied nod. 'I shall tell the Van Dreuse lawyer to contact his clients and between us we can sort something out.' She scribbled a note on a pad lying on the locker.

Amused, Agnes asked, 'Vida, are you running your practice from your bed?'

'I am,' Vida answered, as if that were perfectly reasonable. 'I should have the papers for you to sign in about three days.' She dropped the pen and pad down and regarded her friend. 'Now off you go to the luscious Alexander.' Shaking her head wonderingly, she added, 'Oh, Agnes, Agnes, you're in over your head, my girl.'

As Agnes entered the Pimpernel restaurant and caught sight of Alex she knew she was swimming in deep water, at least. He rose to his feet as she approached, face enigmatic, and as they exchanged greetings she knew that nothing was changed between them. The waiter handed them a menu each, discreetly disappearing, taking with him Agnes's coat. Even while she was reading, deciding what to order, Agnes was aware of every tiny detail of him. During their week apart she had wondered if her memory was playing her false, but here he was, sitting within a hand's reach of her, and he was very real and just as she remembered. How extraordinary it was that someone could appear on the scene and create only a mild interest at the beginning of a relationship and then, suddenly, take on a totally different dimension. How beautiful he was in her eyes now! Dark hair and grey eyes had gained in lustre and depth; the shape of a cheekbone, the sweep of a jaw became worthy of sculpture; hands— surely no one could have such wonderful hands, such a tempting wrist! He was by far the most distinguished looking man in the place, she decided, acknowledging the dark charcoal-grey suit, the bold red and white striped shirt, the red and white spotted tie and handkerchief. And his mouth—oh, lor'! She could wax lyrical about his mouth. . .and he had such a lovely smile. . .

The smile was teasing and questioning at the same time. 'Have you chosen, Agnes?' Alex asked.

Agnes turned to the waiter standing patiently at her side and said hastily, 'I'll have the avocado and the trout, please.'

'Oysters and duckling for me, and as for the wine. . .' The wine waiter stepped forward and Alex asked Agnes what she would like to drink. They discussed the choice for a moment and when it was decided Alex conferred with the waiter.

Agnes had the wild impulse to hug him. It wasn't possible, of course, slap bang in the middle of a restaurant, but that was what she wanted to do. So many times she had been taken out for a meal and had ended up drinking a wine she did not care for merely because she hadn't been consulted.

'You're looking very pleased with yourself, Agnes,' Alex drawled as the wine waiter disappeared.

'Am I?' Her heart turned a silly somersault in her breast as she met his eyes and she swallowed hard and asked with remarkable composure, 'Tell me about your brother. Did he enjoy his stay at Ardneath?'

The first and second courses came and went. The food was beautifully cooked and presented, but Agnes found she had lost her appetite. Alex asked with concern, 'Was the trout not to your liking, Agnes?' as he eyed her plate in the process of being cleared.

'It was lovely,' Agnes replied quickly, and seeing his eyebrows rise slightly in disbelief she went on, 'Really, it was—but somehow I don't seem to be very hungry. I ought to be. . .but. . .' Her voice trailed lamely and she accused, 'You're looking at me like a doctor.'

Alex reached across the table and placed fingers and thumb against her wrist. 'Hum. . .loss of appetite in a patient has to be investigated. There's always a good reason. Has it ever happened before? No? Then maybe I'm the culprit?' and the lines in his cheeks deepened as his mouth teased.

Agnes said, 'I think you must be,' as sensations raced from his hand to hers.

'I shall have to find a cure,' he drawled. 'A few questions please. Firstly, have you missed me?'

'I've missed you.'

'Have you been able to concentrate on your work?'

'By superhuman effort and then only for short periods.'

'Do you go off into day-dreams?'

'Frequently.'

'Has this week seemed interminable?'

'Like a month.'

'I do believe I know what the problem is,' Alex declared softly and confidently. 'I would prescribe that you be told that you are looking radiantly beautiful tonight; that every man in the restaurant is envious of me; and that instead of sitting here I want to take you home and make love to you.' He paused, adding whimsically, 'Has that helped any?'

Agnes laughed softly. 'It hasn't brought my appetite back,' she murmured, smiling at the waiter while shaking her head as he wheeled the sweet trolley to their table.

Alex also declined, and when the waiter passed on by he said thoughtfully, 'Of course, we could move at a steadier pace. We could meet every day and I could tell you how beautiful you are and what a pleasure it is being with you, and we could do an art exhibition—a concert or two and definitely the theatre. We could wander at leisure through the city while you tell me all you know about its history, and then, when the time is right, why then I shall take you home and make love to you.' His mouth gave a funny self-derisory twist. 'How does that sound to you?'

Agnes lifted her eyes to his and read there the understanding, the uncanny knowledge of herself that she had been seeking in a man all her adult life.

'It sounds very sensible,' she said gravely, and glanced away as if in thought. 'But to hell with sense—I don't need any more time to make up my kind how I feel about you, Alexander.' Her lips curved just a little as her eyes swung back to his. 'You may take me home and make love to me now.'

'Coffee, madam, sir?' A waiter had appeared silently and now stood, coffee-pot poised.

Not daring to catch Alex's eye, Agnes said a shaky, 'Thank you,' and waited as both their cups were filled. When the waiter had retreated she raised brimming eyes to Alex and asked in a quavering voice, 'Do you think he heard?'

'My dearest Aggie, you obviously didn't see his face or you wouldn't ask. Not that I mind. I don't care who knows. Shall we order another coffee and confound him with our patience? He might think he misheard.' He watched her with apparent enjoyment as she was consumed by a wild fit of the giggles.

When she had pulled herself together and wiped the tears from her cheeks she said, 'I'd sooner confound him some other way.'

'We'll give the matter some thought. Another time, mm?' Alex suggested, and, with admirable poise, they made a commendable exit from the restaurant.

There did not seem to be the need to talk on the journey. Agnes felt wildly happy and apprehensive and surprised all rolled up in one. Added to this was a feeling of inevitability, a rightness about their being together that made her want to touch wood or cross her fingers as if the thought was tempting fate to mess everything up. As she sneaked a look at Alex in the half-light of the car's interior the sight of him warmed and thrilled her to such an extent that she felt a stab of anxiety. She knew she had high ideals and that sometimes they could be difficult to live up to and she wouldn't be able to bear it if Alex did not have the same ideals, share the same standards that were so necessary to the way she wanted to live her life.

Alex turned his head and smiled at her, lifting his hand from the wheel and holding it out for her to slip hers into it. She returned the smile and caught her breath with the longing for him. The strength of this longing was built upon more than mere physical needs. She not only wanted to know his body, to be needed by him, to become part of him, she also wanted to explore his mind, to be told his dreams and aspirations, share his fears. She wanted to be asked and be able to give the same of herself in return.

'This is it,' she said, as they turned into her road. 'The one with the window-box and wrought-iron railings.'

'Edinburgh is still a mystery to me,' admitted Alex, pulling to a halt. 'My best friend is the city's street guide.'

As he followed her into the sitting-room of her apartment he asked, 'Is this all your doing?' and when she said that it was he began to walk round slowly, gazing thoughtfully at the various pictures

on the walls, at the photographs of her parents on
the bureau top, pausing longer at the one of four
laughing young people in a rowing boat, three of
whom were easily recognisable as being Stuart,
Jean and Agnes. 'Is this Ian Cameron?' Alex
asked, and when Agnes, in the act of shrugging
off her coat, paused and intimated by a quick nod
of the head that he was right, he remained silent
for some seconds, staring at the photograph, and
then turned away.

'Can I get you a drink, Alex? I do have a bottle
of rather good champagne I was saving for a
special occasion.'

'I can't think,' said Alex, 'of anything more
special than this.'

How special, even in her wildest imaginings,
Agnes could never have guessed. There were to
be no embarrassed fumblings or awkwardness;
their discovery of each other was to be natural
with a shared desire to please, charged with
infinite delicacy and mutual generosity.

The silk dress dropped to the floor with barely
a murmur, revealing a cream slip edged with
exquisite lace. The charcoal-grey suit jacket was
eased off shoulders and down arms and draped
across the nearest chair. The red tie was pulled
loose and followed the jacket, and the shirt, which
Agnes carefully unbuttoned, followed the tie.

Why was it that she suddenly felt shy when his
eyes gravely regarded her? She knew it was ridiculous, for Alex had already seen her naked when

she had been bathing at the waterfall. But somehow, standing in her slip, she felt vulnerable. Did
all men appear to be stronger, more masculine,
when stripped to the waist, she wondered, acutely
aware of a chest dark with body hair, and the
curves of shoulders and the swell of upper arms.
He even seemed taller. Her eyes lifted to his face
with some of the vulnerability echoed there.

Alex put his hands either side of her face and
lifted her hair from the sweep of her neck. 'This is
where you have such an advantage,' he said
whimsically. 'You would look beautiful in whatever you were wearing, but we poor men merely
look ridiculous by the time we get down to our
socks.'

Agnes was tingling where his flesh touched
hers and a shiver sneaked its way deep inside her.
She felt a bubble of laughter begin to form and the
vulnerability was swept away by delight. She had
always thought that making love could be filled
with laughter as well as with passion and knew,
with sweet certainty, that she had never met
anyone like Alex before. Her mouth struggled not
to smile, for it seemed that the subject was to be
treated with due gravity.

'It's such a problem,' explained Alex seriously,
his lips making a pathway down the side of her
neck and lingering in the soft hollow of her
shoulder. 'Socks and shoes off first, or trousers?'
His breath was warm on her cheek as his mouth
sought hers. He kissed her, first gently and then

more demanding, asking and receiving a response, and his hands smoothed their way across her back and down to the swelling curve of her buttocks, his palms cupping them, pressing her close, bringing their bodies—the one soft and rounded, the other lean with suppressed strength—to fit and merge and mould so that chest was against breast, belly against belly and thigh against thigh.

With the whole of her body alive to his touch, Agnes murmured breathlessly, 'I suggest socks and shoes first,' and she lifted her hands, running them up his arms and across his shoulders to the nape of his neck, her fingers thrusting through his hair, bringing his head down so that she could kiss the corners of his mouth—something she had long been promising herself.

'Socks and shoes it is,' agreed Alex, making no attempt to do anything about it, being more intent on other things. A shoulder, a smooth slender arm, the swell of satin breasts, all were explored, and when it became necessary to have flesh against flesh totally, only then did the pile of discarded clothing grow, and nothing was ludicrous and everything was wonderful.

Waking slowly the next morning, Agnes found Alex watching her. He gave her his slow, lazy smile and happiness swept over her and she found herself beaming back and they lay there, smiling into each other's eyes, not speaking.

Then Alex drew her to him, saying, 'How beautiful you are, Aggie.' He took a handful of her hair and clenched his fist so that she couldn't escape. 'I've been lying here, trying to count how many different shades of colour are in this.' He opened his hand and the mass of tangled curls fell out. 'I've gone through all the obvious—buttercup, topaz, honey, pearl, saffron, silver. . .and am considering ivory, gold, daffodil and even marmalade!

'And I've been wondering,' said Agnes, leaning up on one elbow and tracing the deep crags down his cheeks, finishing with the hint of a cleft in his chin, 'how someone so lean as you are can have dimples.'

Alex threw back his head and gave a delighted bark of laughter. 'I do not have dimples!'

'And I think that *you* are beautiful too,' she told him slowly, her voice low in her throat.

With a burst of energy, Alex swung her over and reversed their positions, and, with a roughness in his voice, he said, 'How about two beautiful people becoming one?'

The next two weeks flew by and were so incredibly happy ones that Agnes found herself living for the hours they spent together. She worked hard in the mornings so that she could play in the afternoons and evenings. She had never felt like this before, not during the brief relationships she had had in the past that had fizzled out for various reasons, and not with Ian, for how could a teenage romance possibly compare to this? Where the participants were a man and woman mature and well versed in the shortcomings of the human race, making no promises, taking nothing for granted, living each day in a discovery of self and partner, cautiously asking for nothing that was not possible to give.

The sun seemed to shine even when the clouds were grey with rain. They were caught up in a bubble of happiness as they laughed, argued, talked and made love. They explored Edinburgh intimately, as Alex had promised. A small Greek restaurant, tucked away in one of the back streets, became 'their' place and the owner himself would welcome them and beam his delight in receiving their patronage. A romantic song came out of retirement and became 'their' song and they would hum or sing its tune and grin foolishly at each other, renouncing sanity and prudence, believing that they were together for that once in a lifetime, in the words of the song.

Vida Hope left hospital, and, when she finally reached Agnes by telephone, said, 'You're as difficult to get hold of these days as it is to find Mr Right! What's the point of having an answering machine if you never take any notice of the messages left on it! How are you, Agnes? Still in love?'

'Still in love,' replied Agnes, smiling into the phone.

'Ah, well, maybe Mr Right isn't out of reach. There's hope for me yet. Now then, Agnes, I've been in touch with the Van Dreuse people. I want you to sign some papers. Have you found anywhere to live yet?'

Guiltily, Agnes admitted that she hadn't. 'I've been awfully busy, Vida,' she added, by way of an excuse.

'Humph! I bet you have,' Vida returned drily. 'Get cracking, Agnes. You have until the end of October. And don't forget I've yet to meet your Alexander.'

Agnes made some half-hearted attempts at scanning the paper for a new apartment, but she refused to waste what time she and Alex had together. As it was she was trying to cram a day's work into the morning and a couple of times she had the bright idea of taking him round to the house in Regent Square that she was doing up. She chose a day when the agent wasn't there and enjoyed explaining what she intended doing to the place. Alex showed a satisfying interest and asked pertinent questions that told her he understood what she was aiming for. She knew they couldn't carry on for much longer seeing each other like this. It would all changed when Alex took up his post at the hospital, so that it was unthinkable not to take advantage of this precious bonus of time.

Alex was staying at an apartment loaned to him by a fellow medic who was in America for a year. It was, Alex explained, a stop-gap, but it suited him for the moment and was conveniently placed both for the hospital and the university. Agnes groaned in disgust at the décor and told Alex that she would try and ignore it for his sake.

It had to be agreed that Alex's place was the more convenient and nearer to the centre of the city, and sometimes, if they were out late, Agnes stayed over.

They were having breakfast in bed, enjoying their third weekend together. The Sunday paper had been shared between them and the tray was placed at the foot of the bed. Toast and marmalade had been consumed and they were well into their second cup of coffee when the sound of the front door shutting made Alex lift his head sharply, frowning. Two seconds later the bedroom door opened and Barnaby walked in. There was a shocked silence, then he gave them a horrified look, a strangled exclamation issued from his lips and he hastily backed out, red-faced.

'Don't you ever bloody well knock?' roared Alex at the closed door, while Agnes, clad in Alex's white towelling dressing-gown as she sat crossed-legged reading the arts pages, burst into giggles, mostly for the outraged look on Alex's face, finally exploding into helpless peals of laughter which she smothered in the pillow.

With a muttered oath, Alex flung back the bedclothes, thrust on a pair of jeans over his bare limbs and hot-footed it to the door, which he wrenched open.

He said to his brother, 'If you want a coffee

you'll have to fetch a cup,' and, leaving the door open, he walked back to the bed and sat on top, leaning back against the headboard, legs crossed at the ankles, and picked up his share of the paper again.

Barnaby hesitated, his eyes going to Agnes as though he needed to check that he really was seeing her in his brother's bed. He gave her a mournful grimace and disappeared from view and she heard him to into the kitchen, returning to pause at the door, cup in hand.

Agnes took pity on him and said encouragingly, 'Come on in, Barnaby. How are you? Alex tells me you've been home to Canada since I saw you last.' She lifted the coffee-pot and he crossed the space between them, offering his cup.

'Hello, Agnes,' Barnaby said awkwardly. 'I'm fine, I guess.' He stopped and then said in a rush, 'Hell, I'm really sorry, bursting in on you like this. I didn't think——'

'You never bloody well do,' interrupted Alex without looking up from the page.

'That's not fair,' protested Barnaby weakly. 'You gave me a spare key——'

'Which I'll have back.'

'And said I could come any time——'

'So long as you rang first.'

'Yes, well, I should have. I'm sorry, Zander. I've just got in from the airport, you see, and I thought you'd like the news from home.' He grimaced, eyeing his brother's stony face dismally.

'Ah, give me a break, Zander,' and he rubbed the back of his neck a little wearily.

'Yes, do give him a break, Zander,' coaxed Agnes.

Alex lifted his head, eyed them both for some penetrating seconds and replied heavily, 'I suppose it could have been worse.'

Agnes bit back a yelp of laughter as her imagination took over.

'Do you want anything to eat?' Alex asked.

'No, really, thanks, coffee is fine. I was fed on the plane.' Barnaby pulled a chair over and sat down, trying not to notice the signs of female occupation in the room.

Alex glanced up from the page. 'How are the parents?'

'Great. Glad to see me, I'm happy to say.'

'Good.' Alex tossed aside the paper and swung his legs off the bed, standing up and eyeing his brother sardonically. 'I'm about to shower. I take it I'll be uninterrupted?'

Barnaby, seeing something in the grey eyes that was reassuring, grinned weakly. When Alex left the room, he turned to Agnes, saying apologetically, 'I really am sorry, Agnes. I didn't dream that Alex. . . I mean, the idea never entered my head that. . .' He stopped and started again. 'He never gave any indication at Ardneath that you and he. . .' He thrust fingers through his hair and confessed with a small laugh, 'I feel a bit winded. It's such a surprise.'

'A surprise that Alex has a female in his bed?' Agnes queried, amused.

'Good God, no!'

'Then maybe I'm the surprise? You don't think I'm Alex's type?'

'Oh, lord, I seem forever to be putting my foot in it. No, not that either. Alex hasn't got a type. Well, he might have, but he keeps his women very much to himself. The way he does most things. No, to be truthful, I did wonder if Nadine had come back on the scene, but obviously I'm wrong.' Barnaby rose abruptly and walked uneasily to the door, saying, 'Will you excuse me, Agnes? I've remembered something important I have to tell Zander before I go. I guess I'll be seeing you around.' He threw her a quick smile before disappearing in the direction of the bathroom.

Agnes grinned to herself, imagining Alex's face when Barnaby invaded his territory. It must be important, she thought, and then she began to consider Nadine Cartier.

When she heard the front door bang some minutes later she went in search of Alex. He had a towel wrapped round his middle and his hair was wet and attractively tousled. He was staring down at the tiled floor with a thoughtful expression on his face. He looked up as she entered and she went to him and put her arms round his waist, laughing a little as she said, 'Poor

Barnaby, what a shock we gave him. His face was so funny.'

'It was, wasn't it?' agreed Alex. 'Thanks for taking it so well.'

'My pleasure,' Agnes said gravely, her eyes laughing.

He gave her an answering rueful smile. 'Have you found anywhere to live yet?' He took another towel from the rail and roughly wiped the drops of water from his face that were falling spasmodically from his hair.

'Since that lecture you gave me the other night about being there on my own I've kept an eye open and asked around.'

She paused, searching his face, a little puzzled by his stillness. 'Is something wrong, Alex?'

He gave a quick smile. 'Barny has just dropped a small bombshell that needs thinking about,' he replied. 'Nothing that can't be sorted out.' He began to slip the bathrobe slowly down her arms, putting his lips to the valley of her throat. 'Can I tempt you into the shower, Aggie?' he murmured.

'I thought you'd never ask,' said Agnes.

CHAPTER EIGHT

'LET's have some fun tonight, Aggie.' Alex's voice came over the line. 'Put on your glad rags and we'll do the town. But I've a family business meeting this afternoon that I can't get out of and I'll be pushed for time. Can you come round here, say, eightish?'

'Yes, of course I can. Oh, and Alex, someone rang me today with news of an apartment for me to look at and if it's OK I shall take it. It's reasonably priced and not too far out.'

'Ah, good. Don't rush into taking something that isn't totally what you want, will you, just for the sake of getting out? Maybe I'd better come along with you and vet it.'

'I'll hold you to that,' warned Agnes, smiling.

'It's a date. Right. I'd better go. I seem to be fighting the clock today. I'll see you tonight, Aggie, love. . .'

Agnes replaced the phone and stood staring at it for some moments. Aggie, love. . . Life, she decided, with mounting pleasure and exhilaration, was wonderful.

She splashed out on a new dress. Her mood was flirty, fun-loving and feminine. To hell with the cost was her maxim as she walked into an exclusive dress shop on Princes Street, coming out an hour later carrying a shiny carrier in which was a flattering number in cerise and black, fancy patterned black stockings, frivolous black underwear and a pair of stylish cerise shoes.

She rang Alex's doorbell a little earlier than intended and waited, trying to contain her eagerness, hugging to her the knowledge of him in her mind's eye; the feel of him, the look of him, his voice on the telephone those few hours previous. Aggie, love. . .

She was blowed if she was going to hide how happy she was, and oh, she was happy! Sneaky little wonderings were beginning to creep into her subconscious, challenging the status quo; insidious ideas provoking thoughts and daydreams of a future together. These daydreams were against the rules of the game but every instinct told her that Alex could become very important to her total happiness; that she cared deeply that he should become part of her future. And she didn't think, in her more optimistic moments, that she was fooling herself by thinking her instincts were reciprocated.

Time would tell, the sensible side of her would say, and mostly she listened to the prudent advice, but just now and then her impulsive streak would jab a daring finger at prudence.

She rang the bell again, wondering what Alex had planned for their evening together. She had

her own contribution and grinned, thinking about
the provocative black silk next to her skin.

The hall light came on and her grip tightened
on the flat packet in her hand, enjoying in advance
Alex's reaction when he opened it and found she
had bought him the recording of their song. She
began to hum the tune, singing snatches of the
words.

As the door opened her face lightened and
glowed with eager welcome and when Nadine
said, 'Do come in, Agnes. Is Alex expecting you?
He didn't say,' disappointment was total and the
world stopped spinning and dropped a few thousand feet landing with a dull thump.

Agnes stepped inside, hating herself for the stab
of searing jealousy that ripped through her
momentarily, and trying to hide her
disappointment.

'Hello, Nadine,' she replied with tolerable composure. 'Yes, he is expecting me. We're dining
out.' And put that in your pipe and smoke it, she
added to herself grimly.

'Really?' Nadine sounded as though she
couldn't believe this but politeness demanded that
she should try. She closed the front door and
followed Agnes into the sitting-room.

'Where's Alex?' Agnes asked, taking off her
coat.

'Having a shower. The poor man—I've rushed
him off his feet today. Would you care for a drink?
I'm sure Alex would wish me to offer you one.'

'I'm sure he would, but no, thank you, I'll wait.'
Every sense inside Agnes was alert. There was
suppressed emotion within Nadine that was quiv-
ering to get out underneath the cool, glacial
charm. There was purposefulness in every action
and word and try as she might Agnes could not
discount this extremely poised and beautiful
woman. 'I've rushed him off his feet today.' Now
what in hell did that mean? Especially when it
was followed by an enigmatic smile! And
Barnaby's 'I did wonder if Nadine had come back
on the scene' shot through her mind.

Come on! she told herself sharply, do you really
think that Alex is the kind of man to. . .? She
could hardly think it, let alone consider it. . .but it
needed to be faced, so—do you think that Alex is
the kind of man to carry on with two women at
the one time? No—she couldn't accept that. And
yet, did she really know him? Was this mere
wishful thinking?

Nadine had poured herself a vodka. She was
wearing an aquamarine suit and looked, as usual,
elegant and very sure of herself. 'Have you found
somewhere to live yet, Agnes?'

Every instinct jolted and sharpened. Hiding her
shock—why should Alex tell her?—Agnes said,
'Yes, I have, but I didn't realise you knew I was
looking for another place.'

Nadine took a sip of vodka and raised her brows
in surprise. 'Oh, my dear, was it supposed to be a
secret?' She hesitated and went on, 'I do feel

you're going to get hurt from all of this.' She stopped and pursed her lips, adding, 'No, I won't interfere.'

Agnes's fingers tightened on the wrapped record she was still holding. The sympathy in Nadine's voice was hateful to her. She said, 'You've either said too much or too little. Perhaps it would be better to carry on now that you've started.'

Nadine gave another expressive lift of her fashionable shoulders and leisurely crossed to the sofa where she sat on an arm, leaning negligently against the back rest.

'Very well. Of course I knew about your tenancy agreement and that initially you were digging your heels in about moving out. Barny did wonder whether you would co-operate, and I'm not so certain that I would have, under the same circumstances, but, then, Alex is a heady person to be around and he can be most persuasive.' She took another sip, waiting for some reaction, and when one was not forthcoming, she went on, 'As I know personally.' Again, that all-knowing smile was offered, while her eyes hid their expression behind half-closed lids. 'And you've obviously forgiven him, or you wouldn't be here, would you? It's easy to forgive Alex. I'm doing it all the time. There's something magnetic about the Van Dreuse family as a whole, and not merely because of their status and wealth. I presume you're being well recompensed for vacating your apartment? But then, they can afford to be generous.' She rose to her feet and returned the empty glass to the side table. She tilted her head and considered Agnes thoughtfully. 'I can understand you being swept up by Alex's charm—he's an expert lover, isn't he, and knows how to make a woman feel extra special? No, what worries me is that I think you've lost your heart to the man. . .and that would be very silly.'

Agnes was swept with nausea, followed by waves of alternating heat and cold. *Van Dreuse?* Alex was a *Van Dreuse?* It was extremely important that Nadine should not know the sickening hurt and despair she was feeling. By superhuman effort she programmed her face to show merely polite forbearance as Nadine offered her concern.

'There's no need for you to trouble yourself, Nadine,' she said evenly. 'And now, if you'll excuse me, I'll go and find Alex.' She had taken two paces when the door opened and Alex walked in, struggling one-handedly with a shirt cuff and stud. He was voicing exasperation under his breath before becoming aware that he was not alone. He stopped abruptly, his face lighting up as he saw Agnes.

'Why, Agnes, how did you get in? I didn't hear the bell,' he explained, walking towards her, and then he saw Nadine, and looking, for the first time since she had known him, Agnes thought, disconcerted, he added in surprise, 'You still here, Nadine? I thought you'd left ages ago.'

Nadine gave a small, intimate smile and waved

a hand at the table. 'Darling, I've offered Agnes a drink, but she refused. And now I really am going. Goodbye, Agnes, have a lovely evening.' She walked to the door, throwing over her shoulder, 'I'll see myself out, Alex.'

Alex ignored her remark and followed her into the hall. Agnes heard a murmur of an exchange of words, a throaty laugh from Nadine, and the sound of the door closing.

Alex came back into the room asking, 'Will you have a drink now? Sorry I wasn't here when you arrived, but the meeting dragged on and on as I suspected it would. You'll note we're having champagne—nothing but the best for tonight.' He flourished two glasses and set them on the tray. He gave her a brief but intensive glance. 'You look wonderful,' he stated, with the familiar teasing drawl. 'Just right for Pimpernels. I hope you're hungry.'

Agnes had been watching and listening and over the feeling of nausea was growing a healthy anger.

'I've suddenly lost my appetite,' she said. 'I do apologise for being early—most embarrassing when one's girlfriends pass each other in the hall.'

Bottle poised for de-corking, Alex was alerted first by her tone and then by the words themselves. He frowned. 'Agnes, what has Nadine been telling you?'

'Enough to make me realise what a bastard you are. You needn't pour me a drink. I wouldn't drink with you if I were dying of thirst in the desert!' On that dramatic announcement Agnes caught up her coat and marched to the door, two red spots of colour blazing in a white face, amber eyes flashing dangerously.

There was a ringing of bottle hitting glass and then Alex had travelled the distance between them in three long strides, grabbing her and swinging her round to face him.

'Now just wait one goddamned minute!' he demanded. 'What the hell's going on?' He searched her face, taking in the suppressed anger that could explode any minute. 'OK. Hold everything. Let's not go jumping to conclusions. Nadine has obviously said something that has upset you. You will tell me what it is and I shall do my best to treat it seriously, but, honestly, I don't know whether to shake you or kiss some sense into you.'

While he was talking Agnes was consumed with the humiliating hunger for melting in his arms, of being kissed and comforted and told that Nadine was lying. But deep down she knew that Nadine was not lying. She had been too confident. And if she had not been lying about Van Dreuse perhaps her insinuations regarding Alex and herself were based on truth.

'Don't touch me!' Agnes burst out passionately and Alex's face, which up to that point had been showing laughing disbelief, was now wiped clean of all expression and his eyes narrowed and around his mouth the flesh paled.

'You'd better tell me what this is all about, Aggie.'

'Oh, I shall. And don't *ever* call me Aggie again, do you hear?'

'I hear.' His hands dropped from her arms. He went on slowly feeling his way with words, 'You think that Nadine and I. . .' and here his mouth twisted into a cynical smile '. . .are lovers. You don't have a very high opinion of me, do you, Agnes?'

She gave a short bitter laugh. 'I'm a trusting soul, Alex, until my nose is rubbed right in it.' Ignoring the jolting in her ribs and the agony in her throat, Agnes tried to control her voice.

Alex ran fingers through his hair, turned and took a pace away and swung back. 'Right. Let's talk. . .' He reached out a hand, to do what Agnes neither knew nor cared, and she hit it away.

There was a short, tortured silence. Tall and remote, Alex's face was as expressionless as marble.

Disdain in every nuance of her voices, Agnes said scornfully, 'Talk? Yes, let's discuss Van Dreuse, shall we?' She watched Alex freeze, saw his eyes darken with understanding, saw a flash of consternation cross his face, and her heart sank like a stone in water. Even now she had been hoping against hope that Nadine had been lying, and was furious with herself for being so stupid.

'A little remiss, isn't it, that I should learn about your connection with Van Dreuse through Nadine? You should have warned her that I didn't know. God, what a fool I've been! Nadine also said that you were good at talking your way out of difficult situations, but you needn't try now, because you'd be wasting your breath.'

Alex said, tight-lipped, 'It would, I agree, be pointless.'

'And you can keep this.' Agnes thrust the package into his hands. 'As a memento. What I'd really like to do is break the bloody thing over your head!' She pushed past him and stalked, stiff-legged and racked with severe tremblings inside, to the front door. When she reached it, she swung round and saw that he hadn't moved. Damn him, why did he still have a powerful effect on her while she was hating him? She wrenched at the lock. 'You can keep your lousy Van Dreuse money. I'll be out of the building by Friday,' she flung over her shoulder, and then made her escape.

Luckily Vida was at home. She took one look at Agnes's face and said, 'You look terrible. What's happened?'

'Vida, could we go to your office and have a look at the Van Dreuse papers? I know it's a bit much to ask, but——'

'It isn't, but there's no need to go to the office, I brought them home with me to look at tonight. You're signing the final easement papers tomorrow, had you forgotten?' Vida led the way into the study.

'I hadn't forgotten, but I'm not signing,' Agnes said shortly.

Her friend gave her a sharp look but made no comment on this assertion.

'I'll pour you a stiff drink, you sound as though you need one.' Vida handed the brandy over, saying, 'Are you going to tell me what this is all about? and while Agnes sat in front of the fire, shivering slightly, Vida crossed to her desk and sorted through her briefcase, bringing out the relevant papers, listening as Agnes poured out all that had happened.

'There's an A. Brandon listed as director,' Vida said at last. She lifted her eyes from the page to ask, 'Agnes, is this your Alexander?' She frowned. 'Is he a Brandon?'

'Yes.' Ages gave a hollow laugh. 'It seems he is also a Van Dreuse.

Vida was a tower of strength, giving Agnes house room while she made the move from her old home to the new one, assisting and organising and more or less taking total charge. Agnes was barely interested. She packed and unpacked with her emotions held firmly in check.

The new place was only just liveable in by Agnes's artistic standards, but she was luckily too busy with the Queen Anne house in Regent Square to do anything about it at present. . .and she couldn't work up any enthusiasm for the place as yet. It was somewhere to spend restless nights and in the day she was out and about for most of the time, chivvying builders and carpenters, chasing up kitchens and bathroom units and matching fabrics and carpets to colour schemes.

As Vida had warned, there was consternation regarding the refusal to accept the easement on the Van Dreuse contract. Agnes was adamant that she would not touch their money and no amount of reasoning had any effect. Alex rang twice and both times she put the phone down immediately she heard his voice. She then rang Vida and asked her to contact the Van Dreuse lawyers indicating that she did not wish to speak to their client.

'Aren't you being a little hard on the man, Agnes?' suggested Vida mildly.

Agnes gave a stony 'Yes.'

One day Stuart telephoned. Agnes was glad to make contact again, worrying that after her rejection of him she might lose his friendship. Instead it seemed that he had something else on his mind.

'I say, Agnes, has Jean ever mentioned anything to you about what she wanted to do?'

Agnes frowned. 'No. What do you mean?'

'I wondered if she had said anything about leaving Ardneath.'

'Jean, leave? You must be joking. Ard House is her home, Stu. She loves it there. Why should she leave for heaven's sake?'

'I don't know. It's just a feeling I got lately.

That's why I'm asking you,' Stuart came back, a little nettled.

'So far as I know, Jean wants nothing more than to help you run the house and estate, as she's always done. She's good at it, isn't she?'

'Good lord, yes. I don't know what I'd do without her.'

'Train someone else,' Agnes told him bluntly. 'But I doubt you'll have to. Unless she left to get married.'

'Jean?' Stuart sounded surprised.

'It's quite possible,' Agnes said. 'She'd make a super wife and mother. Really, Stu, you should make sure she comes to town more often in the future and I'll line up a few likely males so she can have a bit of a spree. She hardly has the chance to meet anyone at Ardneath, does she?'

'No. No, I don't suppose she does.'

'And you can't expect her to give her whole life to the Cameron estate for ever, can you? If you marry, maybe your wife won't like an attractive distant cousin living there.'

Stuart's tone was sharp. 'Dammit—I wouldn't marry anyone who wanted to kick Jean out,' he stated, annoyed at the idea.

Agnes suppressed a smile. 'You're a bit of a chump, Stu, did you know that?'

'I expect I am,' he replied, puzzled. 'But I don't know why you should say so.'

'I know you don't,' said Agnes, laughing. 'But you will, eventually, I hope.' And she rang off.

A pleasant October now turned into a dismal November. The Regent Square house was beginning to take shape. The agent was delighted and intimated that her clients were sure to be well pleased with the results.

Agnes was not so certain. In her opinion clients always found something to pick over, even when they'd given full powers. As she wandered through the rooms she realised she envied them and a wave of unhappiness swept over her. She soon pulled herself together, knowing it was idiotic envying a couple she had never met, but the intensity of her feelings for Alex frightened her, for surely by now she should be getting over him? Now and then desolation would sweep over her which could only be eased by throwing herself into her work.

She was at Regent Square, arguing with the decorator over a particular shade of paint, when the phone rang and it was Vida.

'Agnes, sorry to trouble you, pal, but you'll have to come over to the office either today or tomorrow. I've persuaded Van Dreuse that you're serious about refusing the easement, but you'll have to sign documents. Sorry, but it's the tidy legal mind at work.'

Agnes groaned in frustration, gave final instructions to the painter, and said, 'They're a blinkin' nuisance and when I've signed whatever they want me to sign I never wish to hear the name Van Dreuse again.' She paused, frowning as she thought over her itinerary for the day. 'I can make it in an hour. Would that do?'

'An hour's time will do fine,' said Vida.

When Agnes walked into the office only Vida was there and she said wearily, 'Don't tell me. There's been a hitch. . .'

'No hitch,' Vida replied soothingly. 'The bloke's waiting in the interview room, and, if you feel like bawling him out, it's soundproof.'

'It's hardly the lawyer's fault,' objected Agnes. 'I shall sign with dignity and then go. I presume you've looked it over?' Vida nodded and flapped her hands impatiently, ushering her in. Agnes showed the tip of her tongue, laughed, and pushed open the door. Three strides in and she came face to face with Alex.

The laughter on her face died, her cheeks paled and she swung round and glared accusingly at Vida, who shrugged her shoulders apologetically.

Alex closed the door behind her.

CHAPTER NINE

'GOOD morning, Agnes,' Alex said, face composed, eyes speculative as they rested upon her. 'Don't blame Miss Hope. I persuaded her that it was in your own best interest to see me and I gave my word that if you wanted to leave you could do so immediately. I'm hoping your sense of fair play—something you Brits are rather proud of—and maybe curiosity, might encourage you to sit and listen to me. I won't keep you long.'

'I'm supposed to be signing something,' Agnes said. After that first astounded look she had avoided his eyes. He was wearing an off-white trench coat opened to show an oatmeal sweater and neutral tweed trousers. He had looked cool and in control of both himself and the situation. She wondered if she could be forgiven for resenting this fact.

'Miss Hope has the papers and you can sign them. Now, if you wish.'

There was silence. Agnes crossed to a chair and seated herself. He was right. Enough time had elapsed for her to be curious. She opened up her camel-hair coat and shrugged it off, allowing it to fall across the back of the chair as she said with remarkable indifference, 'If you feel you have to explain, then go ahead.'

She had misjudged him. She heard him give a quick intake of breath and then he was standing in front of her and she was hauled ungently to her feet.

'Maybe it's odd of me, Agnes, but I'd prefer your full attention or none at all.'

'You're hurting me, Alex.' Her head was up and she gave him back stare for stare. Inside she exulted in piercing that infuriating enigmatic composure.

The grip on her upper arms lessened slightly. 'I don't consider myself a violent man, but you have the knack of lighting the fuse. What are you scared of, Agnes? That you might have to concede it wasn't all my fault? That you might have to forgive me? Don't worry. All I'm asking is for you to listen. Nothing more. I know, as you do, that it's over between us.' There was no warmth in the grey eyes.

Agnes said, 'If you'll stop manhandling me, then I'll do just that.'

Alex stepped back a pace, letting her go free. She reseated herself, crossed one elegant leg over the other and brought her wrist up to consult her watch. 'My time is limited,' she offered factually.

Alex stared down at her for a moment and then walked to the window and with his back turned from her, he began, 'My great-grandfather was an early gold-rush pioneer. He was one of the few who came back from the Yukon in the eighteen-nineties a comparatively rich man. Some found

gold there and gambled it away, some never
struck gold at all, most either died of disease or
were murdered. Great-Grandfather was a determined man who resisted disease and all the other
diversions on offer. He came home and eventually
started a bank under his name, which was Van
Dreuse. Banking never appealed to me. I always
wanted to study medicine. So I'm on the board of
directors and attend certain meetings, have voting
power, but have nothing to do with the day-to-
day running of any of the businesses. Which
brings me to Barnaby, who does. Barny has been
less than far-seeing in all this, and knows it. He
would like to deliver his apologies some time, if
you'll let him.' Alex moved from the window to
the centre table and leaned on it, hands gripping
the edges, his eyes on her. Agnes looked down at
her hands resting in her lap.

'Barny was sent to Edinburgh, ' Alex went on,
'to set up a branch of our investment company. It
seemed a good opportunity, being on the spot, for
him to keep his eye open for a place for my
holiday before I took up my post—I'd stipulated
somewhere off the beaten track in the mountains.
Barny mentioned this to our lawyer, who came to
see Vida Hope regarding the tenancy problem and
afterwards he lunched with her senior partner,
who deals with the Cameron estate. . .who mentioned that the Dower House had suddenly and
unexpectedly become available. It was as simple
as that.' He paused, waiting for her to comment

and when she remained silent, asked, 'Do you accept that?'

'It sounds feasible.'

'Goddammit, Agnes, of course it does,' Alex said forcibly. 'It happens to be the truth.' He took a breath. 'But I guess the truth sounds highly improbable sometimes. You can, however, verify all this if you wish.' He eyed her grimly and frowned, searching for the place in his story, and then going on, 'When Barny met you at Ardneath your name suddenly clicked with him and he realised you were our tenant. He didn't know what to do and decided to do nothing. He reasoned that you would either vacate the property or stay the full term. And he thought it would be putting pressure on you somewhat if he made himself, all of us, known to you. In all probability we none of us would meet again because you would be dealing with our lawyers, whatever you decided. What he did not expect was to find you in my bed under circumstances that were extremely obvious. Barny foresaw complications, panicked, and told me who you were while I was in the shower. My mistake was not to tell you immediately what I'd learned.'

At this Agnes brought her head up. 'Why didn't you?'

Alex gave a short, mocking laugh and thrust his fingers through his hair. 'I was knocked out by the news. Could hardly believe it. The tenancy subject had only vaguely been mentioned in my hearing and a name had certainly not been offered. And here was Barny telling me that you were under siege by our company. Then I remembered I'd been pretty insistent that you find somewhere else to live—how did that sound, now? Ominous. We were only just getting to know each other—I needed to work out the best way to tell you—my own time and place.' He had taken a pace or two throughout this speech and now stood in front of her, waiting.

'And Nadine beat you to it,' Agnes stated evenly.

'Yes.' The word was long drawn out and considering. He was dissecting her again with those darned piercing eyes of his, thought Agnes, and shifted her position, moving her arm across the back of the chair so that she could contemplate her shoe.

'I don't think, deep down, Agnes, that you believed a company as sound as Van Dreuse would go to such lengths, not when you'd had time to consider it. And if I'd told you we would have talked it through together. The ironic thing is that I was all prepared to lay bare our grisly secret to you that night. And, as you say, Nadine beat me to it.' The trench coat was flung back as he pushed his hands in his pockets, legs slightly astride. For a moment he stared down at her, lips pursed, and then he moved away and hitched himself on to the table edge. 'It was Nadine who tipped the scales. So we'll talk about her, shall we, Agnes?'

Agnes raised her brows and said coolly, 'If you wish.'

'Frankly, I don't,' Alex came back strongly. 'I'm up to here,' and his hand swiped the air above his head, 'with Nadine. But, to set the record straight—Nadine likes conquests. I'm one of her failures. I slipped the net in my early twenties and have never been hauled back in. When we meet, which isn't all that often, I do my bit in the name of the family, the Cartiers being long-standing friends of my parents. She arrived on my doorstep that night seconds after I'd arrived back from the meeting. I'd seen her briefly over lunch—she'd tagged on to Barny and he couldn't shake her off—and gave her a lift to her hairdresser afterwards. So when I opened the door and found her standing there I was less than delighted and no doubt my manner showed it. I had to ask her in and explained that I was in the devil of a rush. I gave her a drink and she asked my advice about something totally irrelevant now. Then I made a great show of looking at the clock and exclaiming at what I saw, made some charming apologies and said I had to shower. She still had drink left in her glass and said she'd let herself out. Presumably she was at the point of doing so when you rang the bell. She put my haste and your presence together and got the right answer. From then on, wounded vanity took over and she played some cards she should never have been dealt.'

'How did she know I was your tenant?' Agnes asked bluntly.

'Barny suspects she overheard him talking to me about it. If you think we would talk about such a thing to Nadine. . .' He stopped in disgust.

'How was I supposed to know that?' demanded Agnes. 'She seemed to be very much one of the family at Ardneath.'

'Yes, well, neither of us displayed confidence in the other, did we? I guess trust is the most important ingredient in any relationship and we were both found wanting. Pity.' His mouth twisted into a smile. 'We were tested too soon, maybe.' Reaching across the desk, he picked up some papers. 'Van Dreuse is a little embarrassed about the whole episode. If you could see your way to accepting the easement from them it would show me that, at least, you accept there was no manipulation, merely errors of judgement.' He stared at the papers for a second and then tossed them back on to the desk. He stood up and said formally, 'Goodbye, Agnes.'

She sat there, chin and eyes down, without moving and heard his footsteps receding, the door open, and a murmur of an exchange in the other office, and then the outer door closing. Vida came in slowly.

'As bad as that, huh?' she said.

Agnes lifted her shoulders philosophically. 'Have you a pen handy?'

'You're going to sign?' Vida handed her a pen.

'I'm going to sign.' Agnes rose to her feet and without reading the papers wrote her name with a mocking flourish.

'Then why the glum face?' Vida asked. 'You've been given what is presumably a good explanation of what happened—what more do you want?'

Agnes dropped the pen down on to the papers and said slowly, 'It all seems superfluous somehow.'

'It's quite a bump when you fall from cloud nine,' agreed Vida, collecting the papers and eyeing her friend thoughtfully. 'Is it over between you two?'

Agnes gave a short incredulous laugh. 'There wasn't anything lover-like in his attitude, believe me.'

'My dear Agnes, what do you expect? The man's no fool.'

'Why didn't he. . .?' Agnes stopped and scowled.

'Take you in his arms and kiss you? Maybe he didn't want his face slapped. Why didn't you throw yourself at him?'

'Because he gave no indication that he wanted to do anything other than explain,' Agnes declared fiercely.

'I take it you wouldn't have slapped his face,' Vida stated drily. 'Here, you'd better have this,' and she held out an envelope. 'It's from the hapless Barny. I suspect it's his apology.'

Agnes took it and put it unopened into her handbag. She picked up her coat and put it on, looping the belt and turning up the collar, Vida watching without speaking. Agnes glanced up, caught her eye and smiled ruefully.

'Thanks, Vida, I really am grateful for all your help.' She brushed her lips against her friend's cheek. 'I'll be in touch,' she promised. 'And don't worry—I'm all right, truly,' this being thrown back over her shoulder as she left the room, waving a hand gaily as she turned at the outer door for one more brilliant smile.

Vida gazed thoughtfully after her and walked through to her own desk. She picked up the telephone so that she could inform the Van Dreuse lawyer that her client had at last signed.

For two days Agnes got on with her life and on the third she reached for the phone and rang Alex's home, only to be given a recorded message that Dr Brandon had moved and could be reached at the hospital, a telephone number and extension being given.

Agnes banged down the phone in frustration. It was just her luck—wanting to apologise and not being able to reach him! She dialled the hospital number in a fever of impatience, only to have an official voice telling her that Dr Brandon was not in until the following week, and could they take a message? Agnes wondered wildly what this

female would say if she told her just what she
wanted to say to Alex—that she was an idiot, that
she was sorry she hadn't trusted him, that she'd
been horribly jealous of Nadine, that she'd
allowed her hurt and doubts and pride to come
between instincts and common sense, that she
loved him desperately and found she was only
living half a life without him. She swallowed a
burst of hysterical laughter and said sedately that
there was no message. She then rang Vida to find
out the Van Dreuse number, but she was engaged
with a client.

Agnes relieved her feelings by giving a loud
baffled groan and went to answer the doorbell.

'Quinn?' asked the girl, standing on the step as
she checked her order book. When Agnes
nodded, puzzled, she smiled and handed over the
bowl, saying, 'Someone's gone to some trouble.'

Agnes walked slowly back into the room and
placed the large bowl in the centre of the table and
stared dazedly at the profusion of white heather.
Such a tangle of emotions were fighting inside her
and she didn't know whether to laugh or cry.
Again there was no note, but there was only one
person who gave her white heather.

The telephone rang and she ran eagerly to
answer it, hoping it was Alex. Thoughts of what
she should say were dispelled as a woman's voice
came over the line.

It was the agent for the Queen Anne house calling
to confirm their appointment at the house later

that day. Only a formality because the clients could hardly fail to be happy with what Agnes had done. Her clients would like to offer her a drink to celebrate the end of the commission.

Agnes agreed a time and finished the conversation. She looked across the room at the heather and shivers of excitement rippled up and down her spine. It was difficult to be rational. Could she believe that Alex was courting her again?

Vida called back and Agnes babbled incoherently at her. Vida promised to contact the Van Dreuse lawyer to see if he had Alex's new address. 'But you'll have to be patient,' she warned. 'I might get him immediately, I might not. But the minute I do. . .'

With that Agnes had to be content. How she got through the rest of that day she could never remember. In the end it was quite a blessing to have to consider her business appointment. Having cocktails with satisfied clients warranted a smart, sophisticated image. The ill-fated black and cerise silk dress had hung forlornly in the wardrobe for so long, abandoned. Now it was brought out again, for suddenly the world was a wonderful place.

Agnes was lucky to find a parking space for the Morgan in Regent Square. The front door was ajar and she went in, bracing herself to meet the owners. It had to be done, but she would get it over with as quickly as she could.

The first thing she saw as she walked into the

sitting-room was a bowl of heather on the small round marquetry table she had found earlier in the week in an antique shop. It was Louis XV and was just what she was looking for to finish the room. And on it now was a bowl of heather. White heather.

A movement at the window made her look up and the man standing there turned slowly round. He was tall and dark and there was a tentative, unsure slant to his mouth and his eyes, a cool, clear grey, were warily questioning.

For an instant the universe paused in its revolution, clocks stopped ticking and heartbeats arrested momentarily, and then the space between them was equally halved and she was in his arms and he was holding her tight and kissing her. They were saying each other's name over and over. It was necessary to cling fiercely, to show by mouth and body, by voice and hands the feverish, urgent passion that was unleashed between them. Alex ran his fingers through her hair and his hands, those beautiful sensitive hands, smoothed their way over the soft contours of her body, relearning shape and form. Agnes ruffled the hair at the nape of his neck and sneaked her way in under the open jacket of his evening suit, entwining her arms round him, feeling the warmth of his armpits, the hard ridges of his ribs and held him close as if she would never let him go.

'I don't understand any of this,' gasped Agnes, when her lips were free for speech. Happiness was exploding inside her, glorious tumultuous happiness. She searched his face, breaking into delighted, amazed laughter as she looked round the room, quizzing, 'No owners from the Middle East?'

He shook his head, 'I persuaded the agent to throw a little dust in your eyes. She was happy to co-operate.' Pain fleetingly crossed his face and he went on fervently, 'God, Aggie, we nearly blew it, didn't we?' and then their lips met urgently.

The distance between sitting-room and master bedroom was traversed with feverish laughter and searching silent looks and then the words poured out.

'Oh, Aggie, sweetheart, how I've missed you,' groaned Alex. The cerise and black silk snaked over her head and floated to the floor.

'Me too,' breathed Agnes, wrestling with innumerable shirt buttons, shivering as his hands met her bare flesh. 'I've ached and longed for you.'

'Don't think you're going to get away from me again,' he warned huskily, deftly dealing with wisps of pale underwear, burying his head in her warm body.

'I'm not running anywhere,' gasped Agnes as they came together fiercely, hungrily, unleashing the wretchedness of the past unhappy weeks until they lay spent and exhausted in each other's arms, their breathing slowly coming back to normal.

'How could we have been so. . .?' Agnes gave

up on the word, touching the deep lines on his cheeks with a tender finger.

'Stupid?' suggested Alex with dry amusement. He angled a look at her and added, 'I wasn't going to give up easily, Aggie.'

'Oh, yeah?' She ran a hand lightly across his chest, enjoying the feeling. 'You were that confident?'

'Hell, no,' he drawled. 'Optimistic, I guess. . . Hoping I could rely on your good sense and my fatal attraction,' and he gave her his irresistible, reminiscent smile.

Happiness and laughter mingled. 'Alexander Brandon—if I didn't love you so much. . .'

'Ah, you do love me, then?'

'You know I do.'

'I hoped.' He put his lips against hers and murmured, 'How sweet you taste.' He lifted his head and searched her face. 'Love me enough to marry me?'

She had been lightly stroking his shoulder-blades with the tips of her fingers and at his question she stilled.

'The postman is rather conventional,' Alex explained gravely. 'I do realise that it's not at the top of your list, but perhaps you could consider the idea—for his sake, if not for mine.' He gave a wry smile. 'You must know I love you, Aggie.'

'I hoped,' she said.

'No man in his right mind gets up at the crack of dawn to pick white heather to lay at his lady's feet unless he's besotted with her.' He traced the line of her forehead, nose, mouth and chin. 'Besotted, bedazzled and done for.'

'It was rather romantic of you,' Agnes conceded.

'Wasn't it just? And I kid myself I'm a hard-bitten scientist who works by the laws of facts and positive proof!' A dark brow rose. 'Will you share my name as well as friendship, esteem and adventure? I think that was what your list comprised, if I remember right.'

'Not forgetting passion,' teased Agnes, and then she whispered, 'You know I will, you idiot,' and raised her lips to his. Settled once more into the crook of his arm, she asked, 'What made you send me the bowl of heather, Alex?'

He smoothed a hand along the curve of her hip and then found one of her hands and brought the palm to his mouth. 'The minute I was told you'd signed the easement I knew I was in with a chance.'

'How horrible you were that day, so cold and businesslike,' she accused reproachfully.

'I dared not be anything else, and lawyers' officers are forbidding places.' He leaned up on one elbow. 'Aggie, darling, you didn't really believe, deep down, that I'd used you for Van Dreuse gain, did you?'

'No,' she said on a long breath, 'but I wasn't sure if what was happening to me was also happening to you. I dared not take too much for granted and I was horribly jealous of Nadine.'

Alex pulled a face. 'I guess I wasn't too bothered being jealous about Cameron. I was willing to fight for you. Memories are more difficult to combat.'

'Ian?' Agnes turned her head and looked into her eyes. 'Yes, I loved Ian, and his death devastated me, but they're kind, gentle memories, Alex, and you have no need to fear them.' She gave him a quick, fierce kiss. 'And let me tell you—you were not the only one going to fight. Even before your heather came, I was going to throw myself at you and seduce you.'

'Sounds a great idea,' Alex said, leering wickedly. 'We'll save it for later, mm?' He rolled her away from him. 'As much as it grieves me to let you go—and I only do so knowing what the night promises—I propose we go out and celebrate.' He swung off the bed and rose to his full height, stretching his arms and breathing deeply. He turned and caught her hands and hauled her laughing to her feet. 'Let's go paint the town, woman.'

Walking down the stairs, bathed and dressed, Agnes suddenly stopped and said curiously, 'Alex—this house. . .when did you buy it?'

'I began negotiations ten days after arriving in Scotland. I was lucky finding one I liked so soon.'

'Before you went to Ardneath,' Agnes stated slowly. 'And the agent rang me during the week I got back from there.' She stared wonderingly at him. 'You were taking rather a chance on me, weren't you?'

'Not really. I'd seen what you'd done to Cluny Cottage, remember. I liked the idea of you restoring the place. And I have been keeping an eye on it,' he informed her casually.

'You mean you've been sneaking in here, behind my back?' accused Agnes indignantly, and then began to laugh. 'That's the trouble—working on a place you can become terribly possessive.'

Alex gave a lazy smile. 'How do I know you'll not be marrying me for my lovely Queen Anne house?'

'You'll not know for certain,' she told him, a challenging light in her eyes.

He kissed the tantalising tip of an ear peeping from under her hair, and murmured, 'I thought we could convert the third floor into a studio,' drawing her down the stairs as he spoke.

Agnes again stopped and stared at him, pleasure swiftly illuminating her face. 'Alex! Really?' She buried her head in his shoulder for a second and then broke away, laughing tremulously. 'You know how to tempt a girl, don't you? I'm glad you told me about your plans after I'd said yes!'

'Back-up procedure if necessary,' he teased, and when the doorbell rang insistently he added with a groan, 'Dammit, who's this?'

'Hadn't you better answer it?' suggested Agnes.

Nothing and no one could spoil the evening for her.

'Not likely,' he replied darkly, moving swiftly through the sitting-room to the window. Agnes followed more slowly. 'Not until I see who. . .' The words trailed and she glanced at him enquiringly. Alex spun round and said with some urgency, 'Aggie, my love, do you promise to marry me quietly and quickly, without fuss, and furthermore go off somewhere without telling anyone—*anyone*, you understand—where we're going?'

Voice trembling with laughter, not understanding but content to play his game, Agnes joined him at the window, saying, 'Yes, and yes to everything.' She peered out. The street lamps were lit, for it was now dark, and it had been raining so that the pavements glistened with reflected light.

'Good,' said Alex with satisfaction, 'because out there is Barny, and, for some reason, which no doubt will be explained to me shortly, both my parents.'

'Alex—really?' Agnes studied the figures emerging from the car with interest.

'Yes, really. I love them all dearly, but their timing leaves a lot to be desired—as you've already experienced.' He pulled her to him and kissed her, his hands feeling her shaking with suppressed laughter. 'However, I suppose the reservations at Pimpernel's can be changed from two to six, and you'll have to meet them some time. They'll love you, of course, but you'll have to be prepared for some vigorous interrogation and probably tears from my mother—she gave up hoping that I'd marry and would love grandchildren.'

With his arm round her shoulders, Alex drew her away from the window. The doorbell rang again. As they walked past the stereo unit he paused to click the switch and music filled the room.

'I'm glad you didn't break your present over my head,' he confided teasingly. 'For one thing it sounds rather painful, and for another I've become increasingly sentimental about our song.'

They gained the hall where Alex slowed his step and regarded her thoughtfully.

'How many children did you have noted down on that list of yours?' he asked quizzically.

'Four,' Agnes said, her eyes brilliant with love and tenderness, her face aglow with laughter and happiness. 'I've always thought that to be a good number.'

'Four it is,' agreed Alex. 'Aggie, I love you,' he declared, and threw open the door and the welcoming light spilled out on to the upturned smiling faces.

HARLEQUIN PRESENTS®

BARBARY WHARF

Home to the *Sentinel*
Home to passion, heartache and love

Charlotte Lamb

The BARBARY WHARF six-book saga continues with
Book Two, BATTLE FOR POSSESSION. Daniel Bruneille
is the head of the *Sentinel's* Foreign Affairs desk and Roz
Amery is a foreign correspondent. He's bossy and
dictatorial. She's fiercely ambitious and independent.
When they clash it's a battle—a battle for possession!

And don't forget media tycoon Nick Caspian and his
adversary Gina Tyrrell. Will Gina survive the treachery of
Nick's betrayal and the passion of his kiss . . . ?

**BATTLE FOR POSSESSION (Harlequin Presents #1509)
available in November.**

HARLEQUIN SUPERROMANCE®

A PLACE IN HER HEART...

Somewhere deep in the heart of every grown woman is the little girl she used to be....

In September, October and November 1992, the world of childhood and the world of love collide in six very special romance titles. Follow these six special heroines as they discover the sometimes heart-wrenching, always heartwarming joy of being a Big Sister.

Written by six of your favorite Superromance authors, these compelling and emotionally satisfying romantic stories will earn a place in your heart!

SEPTEMBER 1992

#514   NOTHING BUT TROUBLE—Sandra James
#515   ONE TO ONE—Marisa Carroll

OCTOBER 1992

#518   OUT ON A LIMB—Sally Bradford
#519   STAR SONG—Sandra Canfield

NOVEMBER 1992

#522   JUST BETWEEN US—Debbi Bedford
#523   MAKE-BELIEVE—Emma Merritt

AVAILABLE WHEREVER
HARLEQUIN SUPERROMANCE
BOOKS ARE SOLD

BSIS92

Back by Popular Demand

Janet Dailey
Americana

Janet Dailey takes you on a romantic tour of America through fifty favorite Harlequin Presents novels, each one set in a different state and researched by Janet and her husband, Bill.

A journey of a lifetime. The perfect collectible series!

November titles

#43 TEXAS
Savage Land
#44 UTAH
A Land Called Deseret

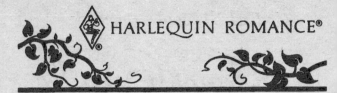

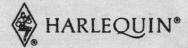

THE TAGGARTS OF TEXAS!

Harlequin's Ruth Jean Dale brings you
THE TAGGARTS OF TEXAS!

Those Taggart men—strong, sexy and hard to resist...

You've met Jesse James Taggart in FIREWORKS!
Harlequin Romance #3205 (July 1992)

Now meet Trey Smith—he's THE RED-BLOODED YANKEE!
Harlequin Temptation #413 (October 1992)

Then there's Daniel Boone Taggart in SHOWDOWN!
Harlequin Romance #3242 (January 1993)

And finally the Taggarts who started it all—in LEGEND!
Harlequin Historical #168 (April 1993)

Read all the Taggart romances!
Meet all the Taggart men!

Available wherever Harlequin books are sold.

• HARLEQUIN •
HISTORICAL

CHRISTMAS

• STORIES • 1992 •

Capture the magic and romance of Christmas in the 1800s
with HARLEQUIN HISTORICAL CHRISTMAS STORIES
1992—a collection of three stories by celebrated
historical authors. The perfect Christmas gift!

Don't miss these heartwarming stories, available in
November wherever Harlequin books are sold:

MISS MONTRACHET REQUESTS by Maura Seger
CHRISTMAS BOUNTY by Erin Yorke
A PROMISE KEPT by Bronwyn Williams

Plus, this Christmas you can also receive a FREE
keepsake Christmas ornament. Watch for details in all
November and December Harlequin books.

DISCOVER THE ROMANCE AND MAGIC OF THE
HOLIDAY SEASON WITH HARLEQUIN HISTORICAL
CHRISTMAS STORIES!